IN THE EYE OF THE STORM

THE ADVENTURES OF
YOUNG BUFFALO BILL

IN THE EYE
OF THE STORM

BY E. CODY KIMMEL

ILLUSTRATED BY SCOTT SNOW

⚑ HARPERCOLLINS*PUBLISHERS*

Grateful acknowledgment and thanks to
Mark Bureman of the Leavenworth County
Historical Society

In the Eye of the Storm
Text copyright © 2003 by Elizabeth Cody Kimmel
Illustrations copyright © 2003 by Scott Snow
All rights reserved. No part of this book may be used or reproduced
in any manner whatsoever without written permission except in
the case of brief quotations embodied in critical articles and
reviews. Printed in the United States of America. For information
address HarperCollins Children's Books, a division of HarperCollins
Publishers, 1350 Avenue of the Americas, New York, NY 10019.
www.harperchildrens.com

Library of Congress Cataloging-in-Publication Data
Kimmel, E. Cody.
  In the eye of the storm / by E. Cody Kimmel ; illustrated by Scott
Snow.
    p.   cm.— (The adventures of young Buffalo Bill Cody ; #3)
  Summary: With the threat of further violence from proslavery
border ruffians ever present, nine-year-old Bill must run the farm,
even after his father comes home to recuperate from his knife
wound, and go to school.
  ISBN 0-06-029115-X — ISBN 0-06-029116-8 (lib. bdg.)
  1. Buffalo Bill, 1846–1917—Childhood and youth—Juvenile
fiction.   [1. Buffalo Bill, 1846–1917—Childhood and youth—
Fiction.   2. Frontier and pioneer life—Kansas—Fiction.
3. Responsibility—Fiction.   4. Schools—Fiction.   5. Kansas—
History—1854–1861—Fiction.]   I. Snow, Scott, ill.   II. Title.
PZ7.K56475In   2003   2002003539
[Fic]—dc21   CIP
                                                                        AC

Typography by Andrea Vandergrift
1 2 3 4 5 6 7 8 9 10
❖
First Edition

★ ★ ★ ★ ★

For the Geers and Corleys:
Susan, Rick, Emma, Rose, and Nell—
I'd stake a prairie claim with y'all any day.
—E.C.K.

★ ★ ★ ★ ★

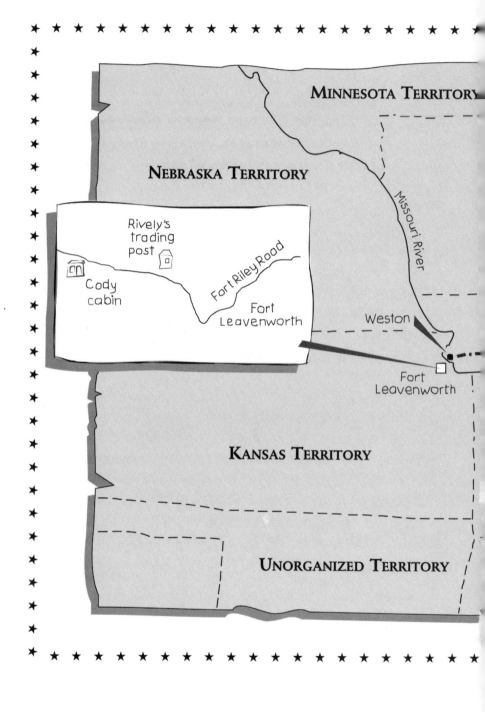

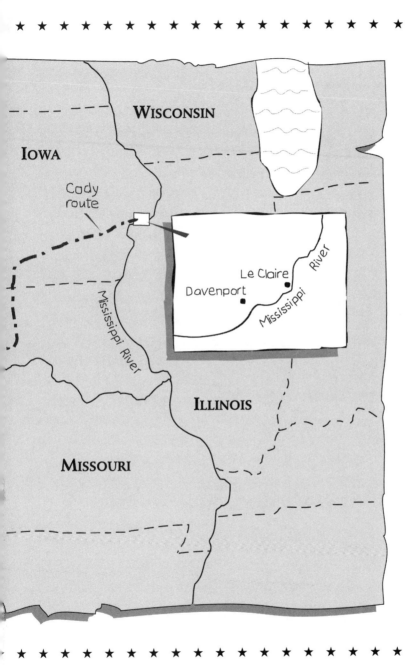

WISCONSIN

IOWA

Cody
route

Le Claire

Davenport

Mississippi River

Mississippi River

ILLINOIS

MISSOURI

CONTENTS

★ ★ ★ ★ ★

CHAPTER ONE

STAY WARM OR DIE

⋆   ⋆   ⋆

They are closing in on him. He spurs his horse on, but Prince needs no urging. The horse is galloping like thunder across the landscape. Through Iowa, down to Missouri, then over the river to Kansas, the horse careens the impossible distance with Bill clinging to his back. Bill doesn't look behind him. He doesn't have to. He can hear the pounding of hooves growing closer. He can smell the smoke from burning torches and hear the swing of the lariat. The border ruffians are right on his heels, and they don't aim to let Bill escape alive.

The last two years of his life

pass by in a blur. The flat comfort of Iowa. The covered-wagon journey across two states. The hemp fields of Missouri. Uncle Elijah's town house. The ferry across the Missouri River. Fort Leavenworth with its soldiers and frontiersmen. And Rively's trading post, where Charlie Dunn stabbed Pa in the back and changed the Codys' lives forever.

In the distance Bill sees his family's cabin. His sister Julia is standing in the doorway, beckoning him to hurry. Prince is running like wildfire, but the faster they ride, the farther away home seems. From behind, Bill hears the riders growing closer, and the sound of Charlie Dunn's laughter pierces the evening sky. . . .

Bill woke with a gasp. The terror of the dream quickly gave way to the numbness in his hands and feet. He couldn't feel his nose at all. For all Bill knew, it had dropped off his face into the pillow as he tossed and turned in his sleep.

How long could the bitter cold last? For weeks upon weeks the temperature had remained at zero or lower. The wind blew without stopping for days at a time. The snow piled against the cabin each night, and worked its way inside between crevices and tiny holes in the chinked walls of their home. Frosty air forced its way up through the floorboards.

Back in Iowa, when his big brother Sammy was still alive, Bill had hated sharing a bed. Sammy hogged the covers and kicked, and made bad smells under the blankets. But now Bill would have given anything to have a warm body next to him. With Pa away, both Nellie and Eliza Alice slept in the big bed with Ma and little Mary Hannah. And though Martha was grown up and entitled to a bed of her own, she made no complaint about sharing with Julia in the tiny room they had built off the main bedroom. So it was only Bill who was sleeping on his own, unless you counted his dog, Turk, curled up by the door at his sentry post.

Was it late at night? Just before dawn? Bill couldn't tell. It was so dark, he couldn't even see his breath turning to vapor. The cold spell had brought the world as he knew it to a sudden stop. The Codys had lived on their Kansas Territory claim for eight months. Until the new year their farm had revolved around planting and growing. Now life was about only one thing: staying warm. Whether he was bringing in yet another load of wood for the fire or checking on the cow and horses in the barn, it all came down to one thing: Stay warm or die.

The thought of horses made Bill wonder how Prince was doing. Of course, he treated all the animals equally, and he knew the cow was just as important as the horses. But Prince was Bill's own sorrel, and the boy couldn't help but fret over him. He imagined trudging outside, feeling his way to the barn, and leading Prince inside the cabin to stand a spell by the fire. That would be something to explain to Ma, when she found a horse in her kitchen at dawn's first light!

It was obvious to Bill he wasn't going to be able to fall back to sleep now. He was wide-awake, and as his eyes adjusted to the darkness, he could make out tiny powdery lines of snow blowing in through the roof. Bill slept in the little loft upstairs. Until now it had been a real blessing. It was a quiet place all his own, and cozy enough when a storm blew through and pummeled the roof with raindrops. Downstairs, the cabin was cramped even at bedtime, and when his ma and all five of his sisters were up and about, there was barely space to breathe in the little room that served as kitchen, eating room, and living area.

When Bill and Pa had first set to building the log cabin, they had made only one little bedroom, for Ma and Pa. It was June then, and the most important work was clearing the fields and planting their first crops. Once that work was finished, Pa had intended to add three more rooms onto their cabin in the fall, and he'd started with Martha and Julia's little chamber. But then Pa had gotten stabbed for his antislavery views. Bill knew he ought to be eternally thankful that Pa hadn't been killed outright. But his health had still not improved much, and the border ruffians would not be satisfied until they hunted Pa down and finished him off.

★ 4 ★

So Pa was staying thirty miles away in Grasshopper Falls, the town he and his partners had helped found. The cabin stayed the size it was, and Bill tried each day to do the work of two grown men with all the strength his body could muster.

He heard a noise downstairs. Ma was stoking the fire. How did she know when it was time to get up? The sky had been iron gray every day for weeks now, and the sun hidden completely away. But somehow Ma always knew when it was time to rise. Bill listened to her moving around for a moment and gave a sigh. He would have to get up now and help her.

Without giving himself time to think, Bill threw back the covers and jumped onto the floor. Even through his two pairs of socks, the wooden floorboards felt like slabs of ice. He pulled on his britches over his woolen underclothes, and buttoned his shirt with trembling fingers. Then came his sweater, and over that his overcoat, which he wore all the time now, indoors and out.

Bill climbed down the ladder, taking the rungs two at a time. Ma looked up. She was wrapped in a woolen blanket, leaning over the fireplace and stirring the embers with a poker. Her face glowed in the orange light as the wood took and little flames leaped up. The blanket parted as she stood, and Bill noticed how round Ma's stomach was. The baby wasn't due for another three months, but Martha was whispering that it must be a boy for Ma to be so big already.

Be it a baby boy or girl, Bill thought, it was one lucky child to be spending the bitter winter tucked snugly inside Ma.

"It's snowing again," Ma said. Bill groaned inwardly but managed to return her smile.

"There's so much on the ground already, I guess we won't much notice a little more," he replied.

From the bedrooms came the sounds of his younger sisters stirring. Martha's voice could be heard, telling them what to do. Probably, Bill thought with a grin, she was establishing some kind of order for use of the chamber pot. It was far too cold to walk forty feet to the outhouse, no matter how badly a person had to go.

"We need more wood," Ma said. "And I could use some milk as soon as you can get it."

"Yes, Ma," Bill said. He wanted to stand by the fire just a minute or two longer. But there was no point in getting warm, he realized, just to go outside and get freezing all over again.

Bill lifted his wool mitts and muffler from the hook where they were hanging. Ma joined him, helping wrap the muffler around his neck. Bill squirmed a little. Here he was, a boy who had taken over running the family farm when his pa had left, standing patiently like little Eliza Alice as his ma tucked the end of his scarf into his coat! Though it vexed him, he knew it was important to let Ma fuss in this way, and he managed not to make a face.

"I'm okay, Ma," he said finally. "I'd better get going."

Ma nodded and gave him a little smile. Bill waited until she was back by the fire before opening the door and dashing outside. New snow had already covered the path Bill shoveled every day. He grabbed the shovel that was leaning against the cabin and attacked the snow. It was no use—it was frozen over and packed as solid as rock. With a frustrated groan, he threw the shovel down.

The cold was so intense, Bill felt stunned. He made for the stable quickly. It was light now, and there were just a few flakes in the air. He wouldn't need the guide rope he'd slung between the house and the barn. But the weather could change in an instant, and a blizzard could come out of nowhere. Once the snow began to fall, it would be impossible to tell right from left, up from down. Then that rope would become a lifeline. Without it, a person could blunder past the cabin and wander around blindly until he froze to death.

It was only slightly warmer inside the barn. The horses stood close together, blankets over their backs. Prince was several hands taller than Dolly, and several years younger. Old Orion, Pa's horse, had taken sick with colic just after Christmas and died. Bill still blamed himself for not being able to do more for the poor animal. But there wasn't much to do once a bad case of colic set in. Since Pa had taken Little Gray with him to Grasshopper Falls, Prince and Dolly were the only two horses left.

Bill put the memory of Orion's suffering out of his mind. Best to keep moving. He measured out feed for the horses and oxen and checked each animal over. When he was satisfied they were all fine, he pulled a stool up by Flossie, the milk cow, and set the pail underneath her. What a shame he couldn't keep his mitts on! But they had to come off, and Flossie's udder kept his fingers warm enough until he was finished.

He stayed just long enough to murmur a few affectionate words to Prince and to scoop up some straw for his boots. Stuffing them each day helped to keep the frostbite from his feet.

Though it only took a minute or so to reach the cabin, there was already a thin skin of ice on top of the milk by the time he arrived. It was a good excuse to head straight for the fire and stay there a few minutes.

His sisters were all up and dressed now. They hustled about helping Ma with breakfast, while staying as close to the fire as possible. Julia was setting the table, and Martha was dressing two-year-old Mary Hannah. Eliza Alice was making use of the time to work on her sewing. Only Nellie, who was now five, seemed not to feel the cold. She walked about delivering kisses to her family, then busied herself tying an old bonnet on the head of faithful, patient Turk.

The smell of frying ham steaks filled the cabin. Bill's insides gave a rumble. At the table, Julia fumbled and dropped some silverware on the ground. She stomped her foot in frustration.

"My fingers are so cold, I can't keep hold of anything!" she complained. "And if I start to warm up, this wool itches something awful!"

Bill expected his oldest sister to start scolding Julia for losing her temper, but instead Martha simply picked up the silverware and put it back on the table.

"Try to remember, Julia, how it is for the settlers out on the open prairie," Martha said with unusual gentleness. "Did you hear the stories Doc Hathaway was telling?"

Julia shook her head.

"There aren't any trees there, or hills like we have," Martha said. "Nothing to slow down the wind or stop the snow from piling. The drifts get so high, some folks' houses are covered up all the way to the roof!"

"How do they get outside?" Julia asked.

"They dig tunnels," Bill said. "Open their front doors and tunnel their way to the barn. At least they stay warm fetching the milk!"

"Doc said every time he gets news, he hears about more folks getting lost in blizzards and freezing to death," Martha said. "And others are running low on supplies, because they can't get to town. Besides which, most stores in town are out of supplies themselves, or hanging on to what they've got for their own families."

Nellie, who was now using Turk as a pillow, looked up at this.

"Are we going to run out of food?" she asked, looking more interested than frightened by the idea.

"Certainly not," said Ma, placing a bowl of steaming grits on the table. Ma had spent much of the fall planning for this winter, making preserves and storing away dried vegetables and smoked meats. Bill knew they had no cause to fear. Whatever else the winter had in store for them, at least there would always be food on the table.

Breakfast was finally ready. The children pulled their chairs up to the table as Ma served the ham and corn mush. Although it had been more than two months since Pa had sat down to eat with his family, Bill still thought it looked strange to have only seven around the table, and not eight. Then he glanced at his ma's face, plumper than it had been last summer.

Bill closed his eyes for a moment and sent out a little prayer. He figured God might be kind of busy with all the folks out in those blizzards, so instead he asked Sammy to watch over Ma and her unborn baby.

CHAPTER TWO

A GIFT FOR A MAN

R ead it back to me," Bill said.

Julia and Bill were sitting by the fire, heads together. Ma and Martha were getting the younger girls into bed. Julia put her pencil down, smoothed over the paper she'd been writing on, and cleared her throat.

"Dear Joe," she read. "Sorry it took so long to write. But I ain't heard from you either, so I guess that's okay. We got a good place here in Kansas Territory. It is real cold now. I have to sleep with a hot brick in my bed and still can't feel my toes when I wake up. I have seen dragoons at Fort Leavenworth, where I have been twice. There are Indians here called Kickapoo, and they are plenty decent folk. I even made a friend of one called Opkee. The best part about Kansas is I have my own horse called Prince. He is the fastest sorrel you ever saw. My cousin Horace Billings helped me train him—Horace rode doing tricks in the circus and can do anything even with no saddle.

"Maybe you heard my pa got stabbed, which is why right now he is staying away in case the border ruffians come back for him. There is another vote in March having to do with slavery and if Kansas is going to allow it or not. Nobody talks about much else. Folks are killing each other over it.

"Well, Julia is writing these words for me, and she says her hand is tired. Write back if you can. And say hello to the steamboats and the river for me. Your friend, Bill Cody."

"I guess that's okay. Does it sound okay?" Bill asked.

"Sounds fine," Julia replied. Bill peered at the letter.

"Looks fancy," he said.

"What looks fancy?" came Ma's voice from behind them.

"Just my handwriting," replied Julia, before Bill could shush her. "Bill's sending a letter to Joe Barnes."

"William Frederick Cody, do you mean me to believe you can't write a simple letter for yourself?" Ma said, her eyebrows arched high.

Bill had to pinch himself to avoid groaning out loud. "I can write as good as anybody," he said.

"As *well* as anybody," corrected Martha, as she pulled the bedroom door closed.

This time Bill did groan, but he cut it short when he saw the expression on Ma's face.

"Julia's got girl hands, like for sewing," Bill said. "Writing just comes better to her."

"Bill, where do you get such ideas?" Ma cried. "Anyone can learn, if they're blessed with the chance. School learning is a gift, and a person is lucky to get as much as possible. At the very least, a body has got to know how to read and how to write!"

"I know how to read and how to write," Bill said, scowling. "I can sign my name as good as Pa." He knew it was wrong to talk back to Ma this way, but honestly, it wasn't as if he was some wild boy living in the forest.

Ma sighed.

"Bill, I'm not scolding you. There hasn't been a school for you to go to out here. And if I hadn't done something about your schooling, I'd be the one to blame."

Hadn't done? *Done?* Bill and Julia exchanged anxious looks.

"It isn't settled yet," Ma continued. "But both Pa and I have been on the lookout for a suitable school-teacher."

"But . . ." Bill took a swallow. "But there's no school here."

"There's the old claim shanty," Ma said. "It wouldn't take too much to fix it up."

Pa and Bill had built the claim shanty when they'd first arrived in Kansas Territory last summer. The shanty had never really been for living in. It was just a little building meant to say "This here is Cody land now." Once their log cabin was built, they'd abandoned it. If Bill had had any notion it might get turned into a school, he wouldn't have worked so hard to make it stand upright!

"But I can't go to school!" Bill blurted out. Ma and Martha fixed him with identical looks of outrage.

"Sorry, ma'am," Bill said quickly. "It's just, how am I going to get everything done that needs doing around the farm if I go to school too?"

"Your pa has been saving a bit of money in Grasshopper Falls," Ma said. "The grain mill your pa backed is doing a good business, and folks back east are hiring him to lay out their claims and help get them settled in. We'll have enough to take on a hired hand or two for the busy times, or when the Hathaways can't spare Nate. It's important to your pa and me, Bill. We don't want your schooling neglected."

Like Pa's was, Bill added silently. As a boy Pa had stayed home to help run his family's farm, while his younger brother Elijah had gone to school. Elijah was now a book-smart businessman with plenty to show for himself. He had a town house across the river in Weston and a hemp farm too. He was an important person in Missouri, and Bill knew Ma and Pa thought his schooling was a big part of that. Bill himself thought that despite his schooling, Uncle Elijah was a hard man to like.

Well, at least Bill didn't have to go to school right now. And Ma herself had said they hadn't hired a schoolteacher yet. It could be months, years even, before they found someone. Who in their right mind would want to come to Kansas in this weather anyway? Maybe he was getting all worried for nothing.

Bill put on a second sweater under his coat, and got ready to go outside. Sometimes there was just nothing to do but be with Prince.

The next morning the sky was a thrilling, deep blue. The sight of the sun cheered up the household.

Ma surprised Bill by suggesting he go out for a walk to enjoy the warm weather while it lasted.

"Shouldn't I be getting to my chores?" Bill asked.

"Chores can wait," Ma said. "We haven't had a day this lovely in months. It can't hurt for you to go out and enjoy it a little."

"Well, why don't we all go, then?" Bill asked.

"Julia can go along with you," Martha said. "The

rest of us can go later."

"But . . . are you sure?" Bill asked, wondering why his other sisters were not protesting that they should go too.

Julia had already buttoned up her coat.

"Honestly, Bill, don't you *want* to go?" she asked.

He most certainly did. He was aching to get outside and enjoy the weather. Who knew when the gray clouds would return? So he stopped questioning his peculiar good fortune, bundled up, and followed Julia out the door.

It was as perfect a winter day as Bill could remember. It felt a good twenty degrees warmer than it had been the day before, and the wind had stopped altogether. The sun reflected off the snow, sending warm beams at Bill from every direction. He had to shade his eyes for a moment, until they adjusted to the incredible brightness of the landscape.

"Come on!" Julia cried, taking Bill by the arm and leading him across the cornfield. There was still a hard-frozen crust on top of the snow that held them up as they walked.

"Look there! Diamonds!" Julia cried.

Bill looked where she was pointing, a wide swatch of snow that was catching the sunlight in a spectacular way. It glimmered and sparkled, and though he wouldn't admit out loud to anything so girlish, Bill had to agree to himself that it did look as if someone had thrown a handful of diamonds across the snow.

"Want to play scouts and Indians?" Julia asked.

It had been a very long time since he and Julia had played one of their games. Back in Le Claire, before they'd moved, they played almost every day. Sometimes it was the stagecoach game, with Bill as the driver negotiating the stagecoach through dangerous situations as Julia hung on inside. Sometimes it was Lewis and Clark, with Julia and Bill re-creating the adventures of the famous explorers.

But things were different in Kansas Territory. Since they'd packed their belongings up in covered wagons and left Iowa, Bill had faced real danger more times than he cared to remember. And he'd found, after a time, that facing real dangers had made him lose his taste for imaginary ones. He didn't want to play at defending a fort when any day he might be called upon to defend his own home. The fun had simply gone out of it.

Anyway, Julia had taken note of his silence and didn't press the question. She probably didn't want to play any more than he did. Though she was still the wildest of his sisters, she seemed much older than she had back in Iowa. Kansas had changed them both.

So they walked without talking for a while, enjoying the sound of their boots crunching in the snow and the luxurious feel of the sunshine on their faces. A person could get by only so long without sunshine before starting to feel crazy as a night owl.

Still, after a while Bill began to feel anxious. Warm weather or no, he had chores that had to get done. "Shouldn't we be getting back?" he asked. Julia gave him an exasperated look.

"What's happened to you anyway?" she asked. "You never used to complain about having a little free time."

Bill said nothing, and Julia gave a little sigh.

"All right, then," she said. "I expect it's okay to go now."

They walked back over the field to the log cabin, which sat looking inviting and tidy in the distance, like a sensibly wrapped gift. When they reached the front door, Julia hung back for a moment, fussing with her boot. Bill opened the door himself and walked inside.

For a moment he couldn't see anything. His eyes needed time to get used to the darkness after being outside. When he could make things out more clearly, he noticed plates had been laid out, and in the middle of the table sat a beautiful jam-covered cake. Were they expecting company?

"Well?" Ma said, beaming.

"Happy birthday!" shouted Nellie. "Can we eat it now, Ma? Can we?"

Bill's mouth dropped open. Was it really February 26? Had he actually forgotten his own ninth birthday?

"Happy birthday, dear Bill," Ma said, putting her arms around him. His sisters chimed in, all wishing him a happy birthday.

"I knew it!" said Julia, grinning. "Didn't I say so, Ma? He really had no idea! Kept saying how we should be getting back to the cabin!"

Everybody laughed at that, even serious Eliza Alice. Bill laughed too, loving the feeling of being the center of attention, his sisters and Ma all showering him with kind words.

"Now we can eat cake!" Nellie cried.

"Not yet, Nellie," Martha said. "Bill gets his surprise first, remember?"

"Surprise, surprise!" shouted Nellie, almost beside herself. "Bill's getting a—"

Julia clapped her hand over Nellie's mouth.

"Better fetch it now, Martha, before Nellie gives it away," said Ma, smiling.

Martha went into the bedroom, and while she was gone, Bill looked longingly at the cake. When had Ma made it? Yesterday had been baking day, and he expected she'd done it then. Only the girls would have noticed she'd been making something extra. The thick layer of jam on top looked delicious. Might Ma have even used some of the store-bought white sugar? Bill's mouth began to water at the sweet possibilities. But then he saw Martha standing in the doorway, and his legs almost gave out from underneath him.

She was holding the most beautiful saddle Bill had ever seen. It was made of handsome leather decorated with small silver medallions. This was no boy's present. This was a gift for a man. It was all he could do to walk over to it. The leather was as soft and smooth as Prince's belly.

"Do you like it?" Ma asked. Bill turned to look at her, his eyes so huge, they looked like they might shoot clear out of his head. Ma laughed.

"I guess he does," she said.

"Where . . . how . . ." Bill finally stammered.

"Pa had it made in Lawrence, before Christmas," Julia said.

"He had it sent over to Doc Hathaway's to keep hidden," Ma explained. "Doc brought it over with him the last time he visited. When I asked you to check on the stable. Remember?"

Bill remembered. The mention of the stable made him think immediately of Prince. How magnificent the horse would look in this saddle! With its expertly tooled leather and shining silver medallions, it reminded Bill of Horace Billings's own saddle. Pa had known! He had remembered how Bill had admired it! All thoughts of cake fled from Bill's mind. He was aching to put the saddle on Prince, to sit himself deep into it and head off for a ride.

But the cake was also a gift for Bill, and one that he could share with his family. He would simply have to wait a little longer to see how fine Prince would look.

In just moments everyone had a fat slice of cake in front of them. Bill picked up a fork and tucked right in. Ma and his sisters did the same. The girls chattered and laughed, forks clinking against the plates.

But Bill was silent. In his mind he was saddling Prince, admiring the perfect fit of the magnificent saddle, then savoring the feel of the soft leather under his legs as he and Prince headed out toward the open prairie.

CHAPTER THREE

AN UNEXPECTED VISIT

⋆　　⋆　　⋆

In early March, when the snow was turning soft and dripping with a *plunk plunk* off the roof, Pa came home. It wasn't meant to be a surprise, but letters on the frontier had a way of getting delayed or lost, and word of Pa's plans had never reached Ma. Bill recognized Little Gray, but the man Doc was helping out of the saddle looked like a stranger.

Bill's pa had a farmer's muscled body and a lively light in his eyes. This man was old, thin, and bent. Pa could cover the distance to the cabin door in six or seven strides, but this man took short, shaky steps. Bill was careful to keep a welcoming smile on his face, but his heart felt sick with worry. He had not known Pa was this ill. And he reckoned Ma hadn't either.

Doc Hathaway was a tactful man. He acted as if the arm around Pa's shoulder was purely a gesture of affection, but Bill guessed that Pa wasn't strong enough to walk without help. Once the doctor had gotten Pa settled in the big rocking chair by the fire, Ma took over, fussing and organizing food and coffee. When Doc walked outside, Bill followed him.

"I know," Doc said, before Bill could say anything. "I was surprised too. There's no doctor in Grasshopper Falls—that's part of the problem. But mostly, Bill, your Pa hasn't been able to eat much or take any fresh air in some time. And he's had some bad chest colds. That accounts for the shape he's in."

"Is he going to be all right?" Bill asked, ashamed of the anxiety he heard in his own voice.

"He did the right thing in coming home," Doc answered. "I reckon with enough of your ma's care and good cooking, he'll come around. But you'll have to be real careful to keep it a secret."

Bill nodded gravely.

"Only Addie knows your pa's come home," Doc said, referring to the woman he'd married back before

Christmas. "And my hired man."

"We pretty much keep to ourselves," Bill said. "We had started getting things at Rively's trading post again. But we'll have to watch what we buy, and not get anything that might look suspicious."

"I can fetch things for you, if you really need them," Doc said.

"Thank you," Bill told him. Doc was a good friend. He watched Doc ride off toward his own cabin. Even after the riding path dipped and Doc disappeared behind a hill, Bill stood, reluctant to move.

Bill didn't like to think that he was avoiding the cabin. There were things in the stable that needed doing, after all. And Pa had all he could handle with the little ones clamoring at him. Surely the most important thing was to keep everything running smoothly. So why did Bill feel so guilty? His feelings were aggravated when, a minute or so later, Julia came in behind him. Did she not understand that Bill was working? Was she going to follow him around as if she were Nellie?

"He looks so . . . old," Julia whispered, as if even the horses must not overhear her.

"That's only because he's lost some weight," Bill said, taking a brush off a hook and beginning to groom Prince. It wouldn't help anything for Julia to be worried too, and it was easier to say something he didn't believe when he could hide himself in a vigorous activity. "His face will fill out once he starts eating Ma's cooking, and he'll look like the same old Pa again."

"Do you think we should be worried?" Julia asked anxiously. Darn it, why did she keep at him? If she didn't leave off him soon, he'd have to run her out of the stable with a shovel. Because the truth, the one he could not give his sister, was that he was shocked by Pa's condition too. How could he have known that during the three months he'd been gone, Pa would grow as bent and stooped as an old woman? Bill's life wasn't going to get any easier now that Pa was home. It was clear from a glance that Pa could scarcely lift a thimble. All Bill's chores would remain his chores. And now they had to worry about keeping Pa's presence a secret from the border ruffians. Hadn't Pa thought of that? Hadn't anyone?

Bill hated himself for feeling so angry at his pa. And so frightened for what might happen. Maybe changing the subject would help.

"The only thing we need to be worrying about is Ma fixing us up with a schoolteacher," Bill said, moving around to Prince's hindquarters and brushing him vigorously.

Julia looked startled. Then she said, "Well, I don't suppose it's the worst thing that could happen. We had to expect it sooner or later. Besides, I need to keep up with my learning. I might want to be a teacher myself one day."

Wasn't that just like a girl? She'd forgotten all about Pa, and now she was going to be a good little student, and make him look bad for not wanting to go to school.

"What do you think?" Julia was asking. "In a few years, if I do well enough, I could get my certification and get teaching work on my own. Bill? Don't you think I could?"

"I'm trying to get my chores done, Julia!" Bill said, sounding more exasperated than he'd meant to. He felt sorry right away when he saw the hurt look on his sister's face. But there was nothing he could do right now. He needed to be alone. She could not possibly understand the worries that pressed upon him. So when Julia turned abruptly on her heel and walked out, Bill didn't try to stop her.

After sundown, when the only light in the cabin came from the fireplace, Pa sat sipping a hot drink by the fire. Doc Hathaway had left a bag of herbs, and Ma had made some sassafras tea and spignel-root syrup for Pa's cough. Though Bill noticed his father had only eaten a fraction of his supper, Pa had sat back and patted his stomach with satisfaction. He was certainly going to be better fed at home than he'd been during his months in Grasshopper Falls.

Once the table had been cleared, Martha put the three youngest girls to bed, and Julia and Bill sat by the fire near Pa's rocking chair. To their surprise, Ma joined them, abandoning her remaining few chores. Sitting on the floor by Pa's feet, she looked to Bill like a young girl. How happy she must be, Bill thought for the first time, to have Pa home.

"I wish you could see the town," Pa was saying. "It's coming along like wildfire. Course the building stopped in the winter. The ground got so frozen, you couldn't even get a pickax into it. But we kept the sawmill running straight through January, cutting wood for new houses." Pa stopped then, breathless from the talking.

"How many folks are there now?" asked Ma.

"Twenty claims that I've surveyed," Pa replied. "And word is three times that many are aiming to settle there in the spring. If this weather holds, the roads and rivers will be passable again soon. I hear folks are waiting to pour right into Kansas. Good thing, too, 'cause last I read in the newspaper, there ain't enough of us living here yet for statehood." Again, Pa stopped to catch his breath.

"Doc Hathaway said the ice on the Missouri is already breaking up," Ma said. "I guess the ferries will be getting through soon enough."

"Maybe we'll have mail!" Julia said, and Ma smiled. Bill smiled too. He'd been thinking a lot about Joe since writing to him, though it was almost certain his letter had not yet reached Iowa.

Julia was a good enough companion for a sister, but sometimes Bill missed Joe with a fierceness that made his heart ache. There were things Julia simply didn't know anything about. There were things he didn't tell her, because she was his sister. Things he couldn't say because even though he was three years younger than Julia, he was supposed to be the man of the house. And the older they got, the more different they seemed from each other. Julia actually *wanted* to go to school. Joe never would have!

And Bill spent much of his day doing his chores, taking care of the animals, and making repairs to the stable and cabin. No girl could understand what that really meant to a body. No girl could understand what it felt like having a whole family depend on you. How big a responsibility it was for a boy. And that was something Bill couldn't put in his letter to Joe. Not with Julia doing the writing.

There had been Opkee, the Kickapoo boy Bill had met last summer. Opkee was lively and mischievous and fun to be around. But their worlds were so different. Opkee knew a great deal, but not about hauling water for wash day, or learning Bible verses, or keeping his britches unripped. Besides, he had his own chores to do, and he almost never came around anymore.

"Are we really going to use the old shanty as a schoolhouse?" Bill heard Julia asking. Bill almost choked with annoyance.

"That's right, Julia," Pa replied, and the look of pleasure on his face made Bill all the more irritated. "You children have been too long without schooling now."

"I know, Pa," Julia said. There you have it, Bill thought grimly. Martha's finally gotten her wish and made Julia into a Goody Two-shoes just like Eliza Alice.

"Any word on the teacher?" Ma asked.

"I do believe she'll take the job, but she's got to get moved here first. Her family is living in a soddie out on the plains, and I've a feeling she's anxious to come east."

"I can imagine she must be," Martha said, brushing some dust off her skirt. "Think how awful it must be to live in a house made all of dirt, without even a window to let the sun come in."

"Her name is Jennie Lyons," Pa continued, "and she comes highly recommended from several folks. Got her teaching certificate and everything."

"I hope she comes soon," Julia said.

When Bill was sure neither of his parents was looking, he stuck his tongue out at Julia. She ignored him.

The fire was beginning to get low, the embers

glowing on the andirons. The quiet crackle and smoky scent filled Bill with a sense of peace. Asleep by the front door, Turk gave a loud sigh without waking up.

It's been a long time since we've all been here together, Bill thought. The anger he'd felt a few minutes before seeped away before the pleasant heat of the fire. Sure, Pa wouldn't be able to help with Bill's chores. But they could still talk, and that would be a great relief. There were so many things Bill wanted to tell him about, so many questions he wanted to ask. For months he had shouldered the burden of the household in silence. Now he could ask Pa's advice, get his opinions, even brag a little about the work he'd done. Perhaps they could sit up late together, after everyone else was in bed. They would talk together, man to man, about important things.

But when he looked toward the rocking chair, Bill realized the talk would have to wait. In the dying orange firelight, he saw that Pa had fallen asleep.

CHAPTER FOUR
MISS JENNIE LYONS

B ill yawned in spite of himself. The bad dreams
had come again last night, and by sunrise he
felt as if he hadn't slept more than a few minutes. His head felt heavy and thick, his senses dulled,
and his limbs slow. Ma thought he might be sick,
and she felt his forehead with her gentle, cool hand.
But Bill knew the only illness in him was his imagination, which sprouted legs in the night and chased
him till morning.

It had taken Miss Lyons more than a week to
arrive in Salt Creek Valley, and Julia and Martha had
gone to fetch her from Doc Hathaway's. The doctor
and his new wife had no children yet, and their home
was twice the size of the Codys'. So they had agreed

to board the new teacher. Now that she was settled in, she was ready to come meet her new pupils, who consisted solely of the four middle Cody children.

Bill was not looking forward to the meeting. Unlike his sisters, he had no desire to impress their new teacher. He'd never liked school back in Iowa. The mere idea of being cooped up inside when he could be roaming the banks of the Mississippi River had made him almost crazy with frustration. His teacher had been strict and never smiled. Turk was made to stay at home. The schoolwork was boring. And since Bill had planned on being a steamboat captain, he just didn't see what use school could be to him. A steamboat captain had to know the river, the land, the weather. None of those things were taught in school, so Bill never cared for it.

Well, he wasn't going to be a steamboat captain anymore. That dream had died as soon as their house in Le Claire was sold and their belongings packed up in covered wagons. And to be honest, after what Bill had lived this past year, it now seemed a silly, babyish dream. Now he had different dreams—to join the dragoons in their smart blue uniforms practicing drills on horseback, or to head an expedition to California, or to be a horse wrangler like his cousin Horace. And even without meeting Jennie Lyons, Bill knew it was a pretty safe bet she wouldn't be teaching him about any of those things either.

All the fuss Ma made about learning to write better! After all, he hadn't come away from his Le Claire schooling knowing nothing. He read well enough, and he could certainly handle a pencil and write his name. What more did he need to know? Bill didn't aim to be a businessman like his Uncle Elijah. He didn't need to know how to write long letters in fancy penmanship. Unless Miss Lyons could teach lariat swinging or colt wrangling, she and her school were of no interest to William F. Cody. He'd just have to grit his teeth and endure it like a man. Like the fever and ague or a long bitter winter, sooner or later he'd be out of it.

"I want to thank you again for taking me on, Mr. Cody," Miss Lyons was saying to Pa.

They were sitting around the table while Ma poured tea and served some little cakes. The girls had put on their best dresses, and Nellie and Eliza Alice were staring at the teacher with wide, shining eyes. It was easy to tell they had fallen instantly in love.

Bill sheepishly admitted to himself that Miss Lyons was something near pretty. Normally what a girl looked like meant nothing to him. But when Bill got his first look at the young woman, with her thick red hair, blue eyes, and cream-colored skin, he had a peculiar feeling in his stomach and feared his face was turning all shades of crimson. He barely managed to say hello and shake hands, and suddenly couldn't remember if he'd combed his hair or washed his hands carefully enough.

"My family lived in Ohio since before I was born," Miss Lyons explained, in answer to Pa's questioning. "My pa had a good farm there, which he shared with his brother, and the land gave us everything we could ask for. But when he heard about the Kansas–Nebraska Act, and the new land opening up for settling, he just couldn't get the idea of it out of his head."

Pa nodded. Bill knew the same thing had happened to Pa. Though Pa had tried and done well at many jobs from stagecoaching to farming, it was the thought of settling wild country that most excited him.

"How many are in your family?" Ma asked.

"I am the eldest, and I have four younger brothers," Miss Lyons replied. "Thomas is nine, Jack eleven, and Matthew and Charles are thirteen."

"Twins!" Ma said, her hand automatically going to her belly. Miss Lyons just smiled and nodded. Bill tried not to stare at the young teacher. What a divine luxury it must be to have four brothers and no sisters!

"And you came last summer? How was your journey?" Martha asked.

Bill could tell that she'd taken an immediate liking to the young woman. He wasn't surprised. With her ladylike manners and obvious intelligence, Miss Lyons was just the sort of young woman Martha would like. They might even become friends, though Bill guessed she was probably two or three years younger than Martha, who was now twenty. He selfishly hoped they would not. Here a fresh face had finally come to Salt Creek. Bill did not want Martha taking Miss Lyons all for herself.

"I know I should say the trip was a very good one, in that we all arrived safe and healthy. But I must say I never imagined how uncomfortable it would be to cross a prairie in covered wagons. There were so many things we never expected—so many difficulties."

"What kind of difficulties?" Bill asked, in spite of himself. He clapped his hand quickly over his mouth and said, "Excuse me." But no one scolded him for speaking out of turn, and really, how could he be expected to show no curiosity about a wagon trip over the prairie? Pa actually winked at Bill, then looked at Miss Lyons expectantly.

"There were four other parties traveling with us," she began. "And though it was intended that we all divide the duties of cooking and laundering and caring for the animals, we soon realized one family intended to do little or nothing but come along for the ride. Several of our oxen became sick and died, and this also slowed our pace. We would start each morning just after sunrise and go all day, then make camp at night and cook our supper over the fire. There were many rainstorms, and the way was wet and muddy, and it seemed each day no matter how far we had come, the prairie stretched out forever ahead of us.

"My brother Jack was bitten by a snake and took very ill, and a little boy from another family fell from the back of his prairie schooner and broke his leg. He was fortunate not to have been run over by the wagon behind. It seemed one or another of the wagons was always breaking down, with axles breaking and wheels coming off.

"Then one day my pa simply stopped and said we had reached the land he would claim. I don't know why he chose that particular spot, except that there was a stream nearby and a swell in the prairie for a dugout. To me the land looked the same as it had for days before. But it was home, and we were glad for it. We passed more than one freshly dug grave on our journey, and we knew we were lucky to have arrived all safely together."

"I expect you'll miss your folks," Ma said, and Miss Lyons nodded.

"Oh, I certainly will, Mrs. Cody," she said. "Part of me couldn't bear to leave them. But it is hard living out on the prairie. There were times I wasn't sure we'd make it through the winter, with the blizzards coming so fast and so often. Sometimes I wish I could have persuaded my family to come east with me!"

Bill's imagination was running wild. He was picturing Miss Lyons fighting off gigantic rattlesnakes, guiding an ox team through a surging river pass, and fighting her way through a prairie blizzard all at the same time. Had she seen Indians, he wondered? Could she shoot a gun?

"Well, we certainly feel fortunate to have you," Pa said. "It's been far too long since the children have had regular schooling."

Miss Lyons gave him a wide smile, and Bill's stomach gave a little flip. He hoped he wasn't getting sick after all. No, more likely he'd simply eaten his breakfast too fast, as usual.

"I'm sure they'll be caught up in no time," Miss Lyons replied. "And you've no idea how much I've been looking forward to getting started. I taught seven of the neighboring children last year, until the weather grew too bad to leave home. I've really missed it. There are so many wonderful things in the world to learn about, sometimes I feel there won't ever be enough time for all of it."

Now this was something Bill had never considered before. No schoolteacher of his had ever talked about liking teaching. They had all seemed to think lessons were something to get through as quickly as possible. But Miss Lyons was obviously no regular schoolteacher. Certainly Bill had never seen a teacher who had sky-blue eyes that sparkled.

Bill was beginning to think that maybe it wasn't school that had disagreed with him all this time. Maybe he'd just had the wrong teachers.

"Well, that's just fine," said Pa. "The shanty ought to be weatherproofed in a few days, and Doc's hired man brought over an old stove."

"Then I expect we'll be ready to start classes by next week," Miss Lyons said.

"We can start sooner if I go finish work on the shanty after my chores."

Bill was about the most surprised of anyone to hear those words coming out of his own mouth. Fortunately, Miss Lyons seemed unaware of Bill's former opinion on the subject of learning. She gave him an appreciative smile that made him feel red all the way to the back of his neck.

"That's very kind of you, Bill. And how wonderful to have a student who knows how to fix things when they break."

"It's no trouble at all, ma'am," Bill said, trying not to look as pleased as he felt. He could feel Julia staring at him very hard, but he refused to look her way.

Suddenly—grown-ups always seemed to have a way of knowing when socializing was over—Ma and Pa and Miss Lyons stood up.

"We're all settled, then," Pa said. "And we'll have Nate bring the wagon round to pick you up and take you home when school starts. Save you the walk."

"Oh thank you, but that won't be necessary, Mr. Cody," Miss Lyons said. "I brought my horse with me."

"That's a lot of riding to do every day," Pa said.

"Not at all," she replied with a smile. "I learned to ride before I could walk."

Bill's mouth hung open for a few seconds before he remembered to close it. A teacher who liked to ride horses? If that just didn't beat all. His mind was made up. If he wasn't the best student Miss Lyons had ever had, he'd eat Prince's saddle.

CHAPTER FIVE
SCHOOL

★   ★   ★

*B*ill has risen at dawn and gone through two break-
fasts at lightning speed so he can be at school ahead
of everyone else. He has gotten the best desk, right
up front and close enough to the stove to
stay warm but not get overheated. He
is sitting with his hands folded in
front of him, as he's practiced, in
the proper way. He has greeted
the teacher politely. So far, Bill
has done every single thing right.
Now Miss Lyons has asked
a question. She has asked if anyone knows the capital of Kentucky.
Bill knows! Kit Carson was born

in Kentucky, and Bill has learned everything he could about his hero. *If only she will call on him! But Miss Lyons nods at Julia. Julia! His sister thinks for a moment, her forehead creased in a frown; then she says "Lexington." Bill almost jumps with glee. She's wrong!*

Bill raises his hand. Miss Lyons sees it, and she smiles at Bill. "Yes, Bill?" she says. "Can you tell us the capital of Kentucky?" Bill stands proudly and opens his mouth. But instead of "Frankfort," what comes out of his mouth is the biggest and loudest belch ever produced this side of the Missouri River. Miss Lyons's smile drains, replaced by a look of distaste. She places her hand on her collarbone and takes a step back. And just then something else splashes out of Bill's mouth. He looks down at his britches, his desk, and his McGuffey Reader, all covered with what's left of this morning's breakfast. Then he sees that part of his breakfast has spattered onto Miss Lyons's skirt.

Bill sat up clutching the blankets to his chest, his heart pounding. Just a dream. Not real. He hadn't thrown up on Miss Lyons after all. He was redeemed. He had been given a second chance. It was just about the happiest Bill had ever been to get out of bed. But he mustn't let the dream make him late. The girls' voices drifted up from the kitchen—they were already up! He had to dress and get going.

Normally Bill tried to ignore the washbasin as long as possible. Today he dunked the cloth into the cold, soapy water, wrung it out, and bending one of his ears, scrubbed behind it as if the lives of a hundred settlers depended on it. Then the other. There was nothing in the loft in which Bill could check his own reflection. Not even a shard of a mirror. A man had no use for looking glasses, after all. All he could do was rub as hard as possible, rinse, and rub again.

Next he held his hands out in front of him. He had cut his nails as short as possible with his penknife, but there was still a crescent of dirt lodged beneath each one. Why didn't he have a comb? Bill had always made himself ready in the morning by spitting on his hands and running them through his hair. But now he wondered why no one had ever thought to give him a comb of his own. His hair was thick and unruly. In the back by his neck, it was as coarse and wiry as Turk's fur. Bill raked his fingers through his hair, wondering what a man had to do around a farm to get a simple comb.

"Bill?" Ma called from below. "Breakfast has been on the table ten minutes, and the girls are almost finished eating. You'd best hurry up, or you'll be late!"

Oh, so it would be his fault if they were late? Not if he had anything to say about it. Bill gave his hair one final swat, then bounded down the ladder into the room below.

"I'm starving," he said, his eyes going directly to the plate of molasses and bacon set at his place. "That looks mighty fine."

He had pulled out his chair, sat down, tucked his napkin into his shirt, and picked up his fork before he noticed how silent the room had fallen. He looked up, his fork halfway to his mouth. Everyone was staring at him.

"Bill," Ma said, "what on earth has happened to your face?"

Bill put his fork back on the plate.

"Washed it, is all," he replied, looking back and forth at the faces of his family.

"Washed it?" Ma said.

Julia gave a giggle, then stifled it quickly.

"Washed," Bill repeated, growing uneasy.

Martha got up and went into the bedroom. She came back a moment later with a small mirror, which she handed to Bill. He took a look at himself and almost groaned out loud.

He looked like he'd sat out in the sun too long, then rubbed sandpaper over his nose. His face was bright red, and in some places almost raw from scrubbing. His ears looked all right, but his hair lay unnaturally flat over his scalp except for one thick lock that stood straight up over his head like a question mark. Bill slowly put the mirror down. Julia coughed violently into her napkin. Pa cleared his throat and rubbed hard at his beard.

"I need to get you a softer face cloth," Ma said quickly. "But you look fine, Bill. Very handsome."

"Handsome?" shrieked Nellie, giggling furiously.

"Quite handsome," Martha said, in a way that managed to sound both complimentary to Bill and stern to Nellie at the same time. Nellie stopped giggling.

"Wonder if Miss Lyons will think so," Julia said slyly.

Bill had just picked up a piece of bacon. But when he heard Julia's taunt, he dropped it like it was a hot coal. He pretended that he hadn't heard what Julia had said. But the memory of his bad dream was still fresh, and Bill was afraid he might throw up on Miss Lyons after all. He stood up quickly and pushed his chair back from the table.

"I'm done," he said. "Let's get moving so we don't have to run."

"But you—" Nellie began, but Martha shushed her.

"Yes, Bill's right. It's important not to be late, specially on the first day," Pa said.

Ma was already at the door, and Martha was handing out lunch pails. Bill took his own and Nellie's, and allowed Ma to kiss him good-bye. He tried to ignore the way she was smiling at him.

"Mind Miss Lyons," Pa was saying. "Make a good impression on her the first day of school. Your uncle Elijah always says the first impression is the most important."

The thought had already occurred to Bill.

★　★　★

Ma had saved some of their old school things from Iowa, including slates and tablets, and a few McGuffey Readers. Julia and Eliza Alice carried them carefully all the way to school. They were early after all, and their teacher had not yet arrived.

The shanty had been fixed up as much as possible, which wasn't much. Bill had done the best he could to make the place look pretty, but he didn't have much to work with. Nate, who often took on extra work at the Codys', had helped Bill to make the pupils' seats and desks out of split logs. Bill had insisted on making Miss Lyons's desk himself, from an old barrel. The shanty had no puncheon floor, and it would have been a waste of valuable wood and time to make one. A dirt floor would have to do.

It was a far cry from their orderly, clean schoolhouse back in Le Claire. About thirty students had attended that school, and because of the many prosperous merchants with children living in the river town, the school had been well equipped. Each child had sat at a real desk with a built-in inkwell. There had been a large blackboard behind the teacher's desk, two hanging color maps, and a globe. A cast-iron stove in back kept the schoolhouse warm, though if you sat in the last row, your back got hot and itched. There was a rope swing, a well, and an outhouse. The school had been painted inside and out with three coats of white paint, and had real glass windows.

Looking around his new school, a cramped, dingy, cold room with barely enough natural light to read by, Bill decided it was a definite improvement. He preferred to rough it. This was a frontier school, nothing but the basics. But would Miss Lyons be comfortable in it? If not, Bill would just have to work on the shanty until it met with his teacher's approval.

"I hear a horse," Julia said. "She's coming."

They stood staring at each other for a moment, wondering what they ought to do. Should they go outside and greet Miss Lyons, and show her inside? Or should they be quietly seated on their benches, waiting for her to tie up her horse and come inside?

Eliza Alice sat down, and that settled the question. Thanks to all Martha's careful tutoring, Eliza Alice's manners were pretty near perfect. The others followed her lead. Julia took Nellie's hand and led her to the second bench, and Bill took the third by himself. It wasn't going to be easy to sit on these benches every day. The chairs at the Le Claire school had backs. These did not. But Bill was a horseman, and these chairs would build riding muscles.

There was a rustling sound at the doorway, and Miss Lyons appeared. She was squinting a bit, allowing her eyes to adjust to the dark room, but she looked at each child with a warm smile.

"Why, you're all here already!" she said. "That will be one of the nice things about teaching children from one family—no one will be straggling in late! Good morning to you."

"Good morning, Miss Lyons," Eliza Alice said, giving Nellie a nudge.

Bill and Julia said good morning as well. Then, to Bill's horror, Nellie leaped to her feet and shouted, "Is this it? Are we having school now?"

Bill had seen children get their knuckles rapped, or even sent to the corner, for far less impertinence. But Miss Lyons just laughed.

"We certainly are, Nellie," Miss Lyons said. "And since this is our first day, I'd just like to spend some time getting to know all of you. And I am sure that you would like to know me a little better. We are going to be spending a lot of time together, and I'd like to begin as friends."

Bill noticed that Julia's eyes looked quite bright, and that she was sitting up very straight. He instantly sat up straight and sucked in his stomach. Darn her anyway—did she have to be such a teacher's pet? In fact, all his sisters looked happy and eager to please. It was going to be hard work to be Miss Lyons's best student.

"Bill?"

Bill nearly jumped out of his skin.

"Ma'am?" he said, his heart pounding.

"Why don't you begin? Tell me a little bit about yourself, anything that comes to mind. What you like to do, for example. What you don't like to do."

It sounded easy enough, but Bill felt nervous. He thought for a moment before speaking.

"Well, my full name is William Frederick Cody. Pa says I got a cousin in Massachusetts with the very same name."

"Have a cousin," Miss Lyons said, nodding.

"Have a cousin. Ma'am. And I'm nine years old. What I like most is horses, and what I like to do most is ride horses. Mainly my horse, Prince, who really is mine as Pa gave him to me the first week we came to Kansas Territory. And I like Turk, my dog, and I like the uniforms that the dragoons up at Fort Leavenworth wear. And I like pie and fried ham steak, and also butter. And thunderstorms."

He stopped then, thinking perhaps he'd said enough.

"That's very good, Bill," Miss Lyons said. "Thank you. We have some things in common, I see. I like to ride horses very much as well. And I love my Bonnie. To me she's the finest horse there ever was."

Bill grinned, then remembered that Julia had once told him his grin was lopsided, so he put his hand over his mouth.

"Is she a old horse or a young horse?" Nellie said eagerly. Bill looked at the teacher nervously, but Miss Lyons was obviously not going to stand on ceremony. At least for their first day, she seemed only amused by Nellie's speaking out of turn.

"Is she *an* old horse or a young horse," Miss Lyons corrected.

"I don't know—I never seen her!" Nellie said.

"I never *saw* her," Miss Lyons said.

Nellie looked bewildered. "Well, how can she be your horse if you never seen her?" she cried.

They all laughed at that, even somber Eliza Alice.

"Miss Lyons was correcting your speech, Nellie-Belle," Julia explained. "Not making talk!"

Nellie still didn't understand, but never one to pass up the chance to laugh, she joined in. Bill had never known such a relaxed time in school. Before long, he even caught himself slumping on his bench, one leg casually bent over the other. Well, if Miss Lyons didn't care about good posture in school, that was all right by him. He'd get his riding muscles the regular way, by riding.

They spent the morning talking, telling Miss Lyons bits and pieces about themselves, and shyly asking her questions about herself. At lunchtime they took out their pails and ate their ham and biscuits, and Miss Lyons said it was a pity it was still too chilly to eat outside, though they all went out long enough to enjoy the sun. If they liked, she said, they could take their noontime meal out of doors as soon as it was warm enough.

In the meantime, she told them, it was important

to exercise their bodies during the day, even if they had to stay inside for most of it. She called these exercises "calisthenics," and she stood up and showed them how to stretch and touch their toes and run in place to "keep their blood flowing." If anyone else had tried to make him touch his toes, Bill would have felt downright silly about it. But coming from Miss Lyons, Bill could believe that stretching and toe touching were an important part of school.

After they had eaten, Miss Lyons began to go over some words and numbers with each of them, to see how much schooling they had already had. She began with Nellie. Though Nellie had not been to school back in Iowa, Ma read Bible verses with her every night, even during the wagon trip to Kansas Territory. Nellie already knew all her letters, and could read some simple words. As Nellie bent over her slate, carefully writing her alphabet, Miss Lyons sat next to her and watched, their heads almost touching. Julia and Eliza Alice were sharing a McGuffey Reader, and Bill had his own worn copy, the same one he'd used in school in Le Claire.

He was slowly reading a story about a girl called Susie Sunbeam when Miss Lyons said, "That's all the time we have today, everyone. I don't want you to be late for supper."

Bill could scarcely believe it. Was it really time

to go home already? It didn't seem possible. But Bill got up alongside his sisters and helped them gather up their things. When everyone was ready, they all went outside. Bill took a good look at his teacher's horse, Bonnie, tied to a fence rail nearby. She was the homeliest animal he'd ever laid eyes on. Her ears pointed in two different directions, and one looked like it had had a bite taken out of it. Her coat was patchy and dull, and her back sloped down like an old mattress that needed restuffing. But he kept a normal expression on his face as Miss Lyons bridled and saddled the horse, and untied her lead.

"Why, she's a real beauty all right," Bill lied. "May I hold her, ma'am, while you get into the saddle?"

"Why, thank you, Bill," Miss Lyons replied, handing him the reins. "You are a real gentleman."

She was up and into the saddle in a trice. Bill handed her the reins.

"Good-bye, Bill! Good-bye, Julia, Eliza Alice, and Nellie. We've had a wonderful first day!"

Everyone called back their farewells at the same time; then Miss Lyons nudged Bonnie, and the horse stepped neatly up to a trot. Bill noticed how good Miss Lyons's riding posture was, and how she held the reins at just the right distance from Bonnie's neck. A prod from behind distracted him.

"'May I hold her, ma'am, while you get into the saddle?'" Julia mimicked. "'Why, *she's* a real beauty all right!'" Then she batted her eyelashes and made kissy lips.

If he hadn't just been called a gentleman by Jennie Lyons, Bill might have socked his sister. But if Miss Lyons thought he was a gentleman, then by golly he'd have to act like one.

Even if it just about killed him.

CHAPTER SIX

AN UNWELCOME GUEST

★ ★ ★

The days grew a little longer, and the sun stayed up higher in the sky each day now that spring was coming. And though both Nate and a second hired man, Nick, were helping out around the farm during school days, Bill still had so many chores that he was close to stumbling by bedtime.

It made for a long day, that was for sure. But so far he was getting along all right. Bill rose at dawn and tended to as many chores as he could before Ma put breakfast on the table.

Then he ate quickly and headed off to school with his sisters. After school Bill had most of an hour before supper to work on his penmanship and copy out the passages Miss Lyons had chosen from the reader. Then, as soon as the dishes were cleared away, he was outside getting to the things Nate and Nick had not done. If he was lucky, he might sneak in another hour of schoolwork before Ma made him blow his candle out.

It had been a long time since Bill had had anything to look forward to. But he found that every school morning, as soon as he opened his eyes, he felt a small rush of pleasure at the prospect of seeing Miss Lyons in class.

In fact, the only thing really bothering Bill was Pa. Just yesterday Pa had said it was time for the fields to be plowed and harrowed for planting. Land sakes, didn't he think Bill already *knew* that? He'd been practically running things by himself through the winter. Didn't Pa realize Bill might actually *know* when the planting season was approaching?

Thinking about Pa, Bill had already gotten himself into a bad mood when he came in from morning chores. Everything looked as it usually did—Ma and Martha were busy at the stove, and the other girls were setting the table. Pa was sitting in the rocking chair closest to the fire. Bill knew that Doc Hathaway had told Pa he must concentrate on resting and eating well to get better. But Bill felt irritated at the daily sight of Pa in the rocking chair while everyone else buzzed around him getting things done. He knew it was wrong of him to feel that way, but he just couldn't help it.

Then, before he even had his first mouthful of flour biscuits, Pa began talking about Flossie, their milk cow.

"You know, Bill, it's important to keep that stall mucked out real good," Pa said. "A cow's got to be kept clean, and a cow's got to be kept happy to give good milk."

Bill clenched his teeth. If Pa had bothered to go out and check on Flossie's stall himself, he would have seen it was practically as clean as Ma's own kitchen. But all he said was "Yes, Pa."

"And she'll be needing fresh green grass, soon as it comes up," Pa continued. "Sweet hay is good enough in the winter, when there's nothing else, but when the grass begins growing, Flossie's got to have it fresh."

Did Pa think he was a complete fool? Just imagine, Bill had thought he and Pa would be able to talk things over, man to man. Little had Bill known Pa would spend most of the time telling him about farm things that any five-year-old knew good and well. It was enough to make him want to scream! But instead, he simply repeated, "Yes, Pa," and stood up.

"Is it time for school?" said Nellie, jumping up eagerly.

"Bill, you barely touched your oatmeal," Ma said.

"I ate enough," Bill said. "I don't want us to be late."

No one complained about leaving, though it was a little earlier than usual. Martha handed out the lunch pails as the girls got their coats on. Bill waited impatiently by the door and took off at a trot almost immediately.

"Bill," Julia called. "Wait up! For heaven's sake, what's the hurry?"

Obstinately, Bill quickened his pace. Julia broke into a run until she caught up with him.

"Come on," she said, out of breath. "Nellie and Eliza Alice are already a ways back. We're supposed to walk together, remember?"

Bill said nothing, but he slowed down. Julia walked beside him quietly for a few moments.

"What was Pa on about this morning?" she asked. Bill felt a flare of anger rise in his throat at the mention of Pa, but he swallowed it down.

"I don't know what you mean," he said.

"Going on about keeping Flossie's stall clean and giving her fresh grass. Land sakes, Bill, you take better care of that cow than some folks do their own children. What was he thinking?"

Privately, Bill completely agreed with Julia. And

he had to admit, it felt good to hear her words of support. It would be nice to be able to talk to a friend about his feelings for Pa, how angry and resentful he felt, and how guilty it made him feel. But this was not a friend, it was his sister. His sister, who'd made fun of him twice about school, who followed him around and never stopped talking. His sister, who was not capable of understanding the kinds of problems Bill had. So instead of answering Julia's question, Bill simply shrugged and kept walking.

"Won't you ever talk to me anymore, Bill?" Julia cried.

The hurt in Julia's voice tugged at Bill a little. But they were arriving at the schoolhouse now, and in spite of its being early, Bonnie was already tied up outside. And next to her was another horse, one Bill didn't recognize.

He felt a sudden uneasiness in his stomach. He gestured to his sisters to come stand behind him, and to be quiet. They obeyed without asking why.

Bill approached the schoolhouse door slowly. He wanted to be the first in through the door, but this morning it was not to impress Miss Lyons. It was because he feared that something was not right inside. He stepped into the doorway and let his eyes adjust to the low light. He could see Miss Lyons standing by her desk in front. Across from her stood a man.

"Well now, 'n' what have we got us here?" said a man's voice. It was too dark for Bill's eyes to make out the man's face, but he would know Charlie Dunn's voice anywhere.

Gesturing for his sisters to stay outside, Bill walked into the schoolroom and over to Charlie Dunn. Bill could see his expression was unpleasant, and he smelled powerfully of drink.

"As I've already explained," Miss Lyons said before Bill could speak, "I am the new schoolteacher. And as my first student has arrived, I'm sure you'll excuse us."

"Excuse us!" Charlie Dunn repeated, and gave a shout of laughter. "I'm sure I'll excuse us. That's good, Miss Fancy Teacher. What else you got for me today? Some eastern-style joggerphy and eastern-style numbers?"

"Once you have seen fit to leave us, we will begin with spelling," Miss Lyons said coolly.

Bill moved a little closer to Charlie Dunn, but he wasn't sure what to say. Dunn and Miss Lyons stood staring each other down as if Bill hadn't even come in.

"Spellin'. 'S that right? Tell me, teacher, do you know how to spell abolitionist blackheart cuss?"

Bill took a sharp breath, but Miss Lyons did not hesitate.

"If you are interested in enrolling as a pupil in this school, I suggest you make a proper application. We can deal with your spelling skills then. If not, please leave so that I can begin my lesson."

Charlie Dunn roared with laughter, swaying slightly.

"Feisty little thing, ain't ya?" he said. "Tha's all right. I ain't got time for no school today. You go back to your joggerphy, Red. I'll be seein' you later."

Without even glancing at Bill, Charlie Dunn turned and walked out. Bill, thinking of his sisters, dashed after him. But he simply untied his horse, jumped on, and cantered away. Miss Lyons came outside.

"Well now. Is everyone accounted for?" she asked.

Nellie, who was standing behind Julia, whimpered.

"Bad man," she said.

Julia hugged Nellie. "It's okay, Nellie. He's gone away now."

"That was Charlie Dunn," Bill said to Miss Lyons, because he couldn't think of anything else to say.

"That's what I thought," said Miss Lyons. "Well, he's gone, anyway."

"You know about him?" Bill asked, surprised.

"Doc Hathaway told me that a border ruffian named Dunn had stabbed your pa and burned your crop of hay," she replied. "That tells me quite a bit."

"Bill, do you think he knows Pa is here?" Julia cried out suddenly. Panic gripped Bill. Why hadn't he thought of that?

"If he does, he'll be headin' for the cabin," said Bill.

"You'd best go and check, Bill," Miss Lyons said.

"Oh do, Bill," cried Julia. "Run right now!"

Bill hesitated, looking at his sisters. Why was everyone telling him what to do? Why wasn't he in charge? Why hadn't he thought about Pa?

"Don't worry about us, Bill," Miss Lyons said. "I don't think Mr. Dunn will be coming back here today. He was too wobbly on his own legs to be upright much longer. We'll be fine here."

Miss Lyons looked determined and unafraid. She walked over to the fence, where Bill's old ax was leaning. She picked it up matter-of-factly and carried it to the schoolhouse door.

"We'll be fine," she repeated, giving the ax a little pat for emphasis.

"Okay, then," Bill said, feeling his world turned upside down. "I'll go to the cabin."

"Best take Bonnie," Miss Lyons said. "Save yourself a few minutes. Just give her her head—she's quick as lightning."

"Thank you, ma'am," Bill called, already on Bonnie's back. There was no time to saddle her up. He'd have to go bareback.

Miss Lyons was right about Bonnie being fast. The shanty was half a mile from the Codys' house, and the ride took only about a minute. Still, it was long enough for Bill to chide himself over how he'd handled things. Or rather, how he hadn't. Here he comes upon his worst enemy in the world, a dangerous, murderous man, trying to frighten Miss Lyons. And who kept a cool head and a sharp tongue and saved the day by refusing to act scared? Was it Bill? Not even close. It was Miss Lyons herself who'd taken action, while Bill was about as helpful as a doorpost. Bill shook his head in disgust at his inadequacy. How would he face her again? But now he had reached the cabin, and he had to banish all thoughts of Miss Lyons from his mind.

Everything looked quiet from the outside, and there was no sign of Charlie Dunn's horse. Ma and Martha were outside, scrubbing soapy laundry on washboards.

"Bill! What is it? Is someone hurt?" Martha asked.

"Has Charlie Dunn been here?" Bill asked, swinging down from Bonnie. Ma put her hand over her mouth. Bill could hear the sound of Pa's voice calling from inside.

"We'd best go in the house," Ma said, her eyes anxiously scanning the horizon.

Bill entered last, pulling the door shut behind him.

"Thought I heard your voice," Pa said. He hadn't moved since Bill had left him after breakfast. "What'd you get sent home for, son?"

"I didn't get sent home!" Bill said sharply, letting his temper momentarily get the better of him. "Charlie Dunn came to the school. Didn't do nothing, but he had a few drinks in him. I was afraid he'd come here next and find you."

Pa sat frozen in the chair. Martha looked out the window.

"I don't see anybody," she said. "And Turk hasn't so much as whined."

"Was he alone, Bill?" Ma asked.

"Yes, Ma," Bill said, but his eyes were on Pa. Why wasn't he saying anything? Why was he just sitting there like that?

"He didn't mention Pa," Bill said. "I'm guessing he was just riding along the road from Rively's and noticed Miss Lyons's horse outside the shanty. Went to have a look, maybe make some mischief."

"Where are Jennie and the girls?" asked Martha.

"Still at the schoolhouse," Bill said.

Ma raised her eyebrows and looked like she was about to say something.

"It's all right, Ma," Bill said. "You should have seen how cool she handled herself when Dunn was there. And she's got my wood ax and looks like she knows how to swing it."

"All the same, let's get them back here. There'll be no more school for today."

Bill knew from Ma's tone that she would not budge. And truth to tell, he felt so topsy-turvy that he was just as happy not to be in school today. He was sure that Miss Lyons's lessons would be as understandable as . . . as Opkee when he spoke Kickapoo!

"I'll take the wagon," Bill said, and left.

Bill's thoughts on the way back to school were no happier than the ones he had had leaving school. Why hadn't Pa done anything? Why hadn't Pa even spoken up, made a suggestion, asked something? Had he brought all this danger on them, only so he could sit by the fire like somebody's granny?

Bill felt terrible having these disloyal thoughts. But what else was he to think? It was not Pa's fault that he'd been stabbed, not Pa's fault that the Codys were now the declared enemies of every proslaver west of Leavenworth. Bill would never fault Pa for sticking up for what he believed in. In fact, he was proud of it.

But Bill could not match that Pa with this one. *This* Pa couldn't do anything and didn't have much to say, unless it was to tell Bill things about the farm he already knew. And his very presence in the cabin put all the Codys in danger. What was Bill to make of it? What was he to think?

The question still weighed heavily on him hours later, when a place had been made for Miss Lyons to sleep alongside Martha and Julia, when the supper things had been cleared away and the lanterns put out. Everyone was safe and accounted for, and quiet settled over the cabin like a blanket. But Bill lay for a long time in the dark, staring, until he fell asleep.

★   ★   ★

"They're coming! We have two minutes! Pa, we've got to get you out back and into the cornfield—you'll be safe there!"

But Pa just sits by the fire.

"Pa, did you hear me? I said they're coming right now, and they mean to hurt us if they find you here. We've got to get you into the field!"

To Bill's disbelief, Pa still does not move. He turns to look at Bill, his cheeks sunken and his eyes huge.

"Pa, please," Bill says desperately. "If they come through that door and find you here, they'll kill you. They may kill all of us."

Pa still says nothing.

Bill grabs him by the shoulders. "Pa, you've got to pull yourself together, do you hear? They'll kill us, Pa! THEY'LL KILL US!"

Still, Pa does not move, even when the front door crashes open behind him.

CHAPTER SEVEN

BILL'S RIDE

★   ★   ★

Bill's head felt like a boulder, his feet like lead. The fried ham Ma had given him for breakfast sat like a hot, fatty cannonball in his stomach. And his dream kept playing over and over in his head.

Bill knew it wasn't fair to be riled at someone over something he did to you in a dream. But every time he glanced at Pa, he felt hot pokers of anger burning into him. Right now he just couldn't separate Dream Pa from Real Pa. They felt like the same person, and

Bill was about to bust trying to look like nothing was wrong.

He stood up then. He stumbled through the usual motions, picking up his books, taking his lunch pail, going outside. But there was a growing refrain in his mind. It went something like *I can't, I can't, I can't.*

There would be class until midafternoon; then Bill needed to hurry back and help Nick and Nate get ready for the spring planting. That would go on until there wasn't enough sunlight to see. Then he'd eat supper, and work on his lessons until his eyes gave out. Bill just didn't see how he could do it, with all the worrying he had on his mind. For the first time since school had begun, not even the thought of seeing Miss Lyons made him feel better.

His sisters were walking and chattering behind him as they passed the stable and headed for the shanty. The sound of Prince nickering from the stable, and the smell of hay in the air, caused something to suddenly snap in Bill. He had to ride. He had to be with his horse. It was the only thing left in his life that was truly his, where he felt absolutely like Bill Cody. Eliza Alice and Nellie had wandered off the path a ways to pick some wildflowers for Miss Lyons. Bill grabbed Julia's arm.

"I can't go to school," he whispered. "I just can't. I gotta get away—I gotta ride. Miss Lyons said she knew I might have to miss some school to do extra work now that it's almost planting time."

Julia's face lit up, and for a moment Bill felt relieved.

"Then I'm coming with you," she said. Bill shook his head vigorously.

"You can't!" he said. "Someone has to stay with Eliza Alice and Nellie. I just need you to tell Miss Lyons I'm doing planting work, that's all, Julia. And not to tell Ma and Pa I skipped school."

Julia stood with her hands on her hips.

"Oh, so you get to go off riding and having fun, but nobody else does? Why should I fib for you? You barely even say two words to me anymore."

Bill scowled. "Well, don't, then!" he cried. "I'm going anyway."

He strode off toward the stable, and Nellie called after him.

"Bill, where you going?"

"I got some chores to take care of, Nellie," Bill called over his shoulder. "You go on with Julia."

Julia. She'd land him in a heap of trouble when he got home. But that just didn't matter right now. Bill opened up the stable door, and as Prince turned his head and stared at him with his golden-brown eyes, Bill figured any punishment he got would be well worth it.

Bill slipped into the stall and wrapped his arms around Prince's muscled neck. He pressed his face against the sleek warmth of the horse's coat. With one hand he reached up and curled his fingers through a fistful of mane. Bill basked in the smell of his horse, a smell of hay and leather, of musky sweat, of freedom. Bill stood that way long enough for his sisters to reach the schoolhouse, peace-fully frozen in place and quieted by the kind of love a boy can have only for a horse.

After he'd waited long enough, he gathered up Prince's tack, slipping the bridle over the horse's head and placing the beautiful leather-and-silver saddle gently on his back. He adjusted it, tightened the girth, and led Prince outside. The cabin door was closed, and Bill wasted no time. He climbed into the saddle. With only the slightest squeeze of Bill's knees, Prince set out at a brisk walk, warming up his muscles and loosening his limbs. The leather creaked as they moved. Soon Prince began to trot, and then to canter. Bill didn't even have a destination in mind. Let Prince take him wherever he would.

The sound of Prince's hoofbeats cantering on the earth, one-two-three, one-two-three, one-two-three, lulled Bill like a bedtime lullaby. He fit so perfectly into the horse's rhythm, he barely needed reins or stirrups or the saddle itself. Horse and boy moved as if they were parts of the same creature.

The wind in his face filled his nose with the tangy soil-and-bud smell of the coming spring. There were so many things he'd forgotten these last weeks. How the sunshine relaxed him like a crackling fire after a cold, hard day. How the smell of good clean air and growing plants made his heart and lungs feel full of strength. How the knowledge that he had Prince, that they could go anywhere they chose together, made him feel safe. He'd forgotten how good it felt to appreciate what was around him.

They were headed east, toward the river, staying clear of the roads. They cantered past Shady Creek, past the old smallpox hospital, through the former Kickapoo Indian village on land that was now being settled by whites. Bill thought briefly of Opkee, his Kickapoo friend, kept away by his own family responsibilities.

Prince slowed himself to a walk. They were at the bluff overlooking the Missouri River. Upriver Bill could see a steamboat, carrying passengers or freight, probably both. Back in Iowa, Bill couldn't stand seeing a steamboat without getting its name, finding out who captained it, where it was headed. But this steamboat was of no more or less importance than the hawk circling above the river. It was part of the landscape, but no longer part of his dream world.

Bill dismounted and led Prince to a shady, grassy area where the horse could graze in comfort. There was a small spring nearby where they could both drink. This place would do for a while.

Bill planned to nap. That was his intention when he stretched out in the shade close to where Prince was grazing. He did manage to stretch out for a few minutes, content to feel the river breeze and watch the clouds. But before long he felt restless. Anxious. Now that he was no longer riding, he found himself thinking of all the chores that needed doing on the farm. The day was only half gone. If he rode home now, he could still get the scythes sharpened, split some kindling, and see to the old yoke that needed repairing. He'd had his time with Prince now. Maybe if he went home for the afternoon, he wouldn't be guilty of telling a whole lie. And half a lie was better than a whole. His mind made up, he already felt better. He and Prince headed back.

The Fort Riley Road that led west looked empty, so Bill allowed Prince to walk down it a short way. When he was able to see Rively's trading post in the distance, he guided Prince off the road. As they headed through the meadow, Bill glanced back over his shoulder at Rively's. All looked quiet, and the modest log building looked as innocent and inviting as any settler's cabin. But even as Bill looked, he could vividly feel the heat of the mob that had pulled Pa from his horse and stood by while he was stabbed. Bill suddenly thought how terrified Pa must have felt at that moment.

Bill pulled up the reins gently and stopped Prince. Pa had been faced with a crowd of drunken men armed with knives, bottles, ropes, and seething anger. And he had told them the one thing he knew could incite them to violence. He had told them the truth. He had told them he opposed slavery in Kansas

Territory, now and always. And he had almost paid for it with his life.

That Pa, the brave man who had not been cowed in front of his enemies, was the same man as the Pa who now sat healing in the rocker by the fireplace. Of all the things he had forgotten, how could Bill have forgotten what had landed Pa in his injured state to begin with?

Yes, Pa was weak and sickly now. But that would change. With rest and food and the love of his family, he would get better, God willing. What would never change was the courage Pa had shown that day at Rively's. That would stand forever. One day history books might even reflect that Isaac Cody's blood was the first shed in Kansas Territory in the name of freedom. How could Bill feel anything but pride to be this man's son?

Bill urged Prince to a trot. Suddenly he was in a hurry to be home.

One glance at Julia's face as Bill came into the cabin confirmed his fears. She looked smug, and a small smile played about her lips. Naturally, she'd told Ma and Pa that he'd skipped school and fibbed about the chores. What else would he have expected her to do? He'd be punished now, though with a guilty start he realized Pa might still be too weak to give him much of a thrashing.

He pulled the door closed behind him. Ma turned

at the sound and smiled at him. Bill immediately looked over at Pa, who was shifting the logs in the fireplace with a poker. Pa glanced back at Bill, gave him a nod, and continued to poke at the fire.

"I chopped some extra kindling, Pa," Bill said.

"Thanks all the same, son," Pa said. "I think we're set for now. But it'll come in handy for your ma in the morning."

They had a supper like any other night, save that Pa ate a bit more than usual.

Throughout the meal Bill cast looks at his sister. Julia's expression was impossible to read. What had happened? Maybe she had lied for him after all. Should he say something? Was this part of some new plan she was hatching to get back at him?

There was a moment, after the supper things had been cleared away, when Bill found himself standing next to Julia by the stove. He was practically standing on her toes, but Julia acted like she didn't notice he was there. If he was ever going to say anything to her about it, it should be now. But he didn't know where to begin. Should he thank her? Apologize?

Then the opportunity was lost as Martha began issuing her bedtime orders to the younger girls.

It was not the first time Bill found words failing him, and it would probably not be the last.

CHAPTER EIGHT
TROUBLE BREWING

★　　★　　★

*B*ill is in the stable, grooming Prince, when he senses
a darkening outside, as if the sun has slipped
behind a black cloud. Prince is nervously shifting
from hoof to hoof, moving fitfully away from Bill.

"What is it, boy?" Bill asked. "Storm coming? Got you
nervous?"

Bill feels around in his pocket for a carrot, but Prince
has backed into the corner of his stall. His eyes look wild
now, as if he's seen a pan-
ther in a tree overhead.

"Easy boy, easy,"
Bill coaxes, reach-
ing his hands out

toward his horse. But the animal will not be comforted. He rears up on his hind legs, his front hooves slicing at the air. Bill ducks under the door of the stall and backs away. What has gotten into Prince? It's as if the animal never saw bad weather before.

Bill looks at his frantic horse for a moment and decides to give it a rest. He'll check outside, make sure everything is safely secured before the storm comes. When he gets back, Prince will be calmer. He will be his old self again.

He tries not to let his feelings get hurt. His own horse not trusting him, backing away from him like he's the enemy. Bill sighs and opens the stable door.

It's terribly dark outside, but it hasn't started raining yet. Bill latches the stable door behind him and looks up at the angry sky. He's never seen a storm cloud quite like it. It's black and opaque, and it seems almost alive, like the angry toiling of a thousand ants swarming over a slab of meat. Maybe there's going to be a cyclone. He should get back to the cabin, Bill thinks. Warn Ma and Pa, and the girls, make sure they go down into the root cellar.

But he doesn't move. He stares at the sky again. And with a groan of fear, Bill realizes that it is not a storm cloud that has swallowed the sun. It is a mass of thousands upon thousands of crows. They have gathered in the sky over his head, ready to swoop.

Miss Lyons looked different when she wasn't teaching. It was strange, having her there at the table with them. After so many lessons, Bill had gotten used to thinking of her as a teacher, not a regular person. She took all her meals at the Hathaways', except for what she brought to school in her lunch pail. But Martha had persuaded Ma to invite Miss Lyons to share a meal. Sitting at the table with the Codys for supper, she looked like a different person altogether.

Miss Lyons looked up suddenly and saw Bill looking at her. She smiled at him. He tried to smile back, but it came out all wrong. He quickly looked away.

"You look peaked, Bill," Miss Lyons said during a pause in the conversation. "Are you feeling ill?"

"No, ma'am," Bill said. "I reckon I'm just tired. Had to help the hired men get the corn seed planted. I'll be all right in the morning."

"He does work hard, our Bill," Pa said, spearing a slice of ham steak with his fork. "I know it's early, but how do you think the crop looks, Bill?"

Bill felt startled to hear Pa ask. It was the first time he'd sought Bill's opinion about the farm, rather than giving his own. And as Pa said, it was early. Too early to predict the crop, as Pa knew very well. Even the first tiny green shoots would not be visible for a week. Still, he took a moment to think before replying.

"The soil is real healthy. I expect if the frost and the locusts stay away, we'll have a fine crop come August," Bill said.

Pa nodded and accepted a second helping of bread from Ma. He's eating much better, Bill thought. And the color's coming back to his face.

"I do declare I'm feeling better than I have in weeks," Pa said, as if reading Bill's thoughts. "It does me good to know the farm is in good hands, and my children are getting their schooling."

"They are wonderful pupils," Miss Lyons said. "It's beyond me how Bill takes care of his farm chores and still leaves time enough for his studies. They all learn so quickly. Julia's penmanship is growing finer each day."

Julia's smile glowed like a little torch. Bill scowled into his ham. What about his penmanship?

"That's wonderful, Julia," Ma said. "It pleases me to hear you're making such strides."

"Oh, they all are, Mrs. Cody," Miss Lyons continued eagerly. "Eliza Alice is reading almost as well as Julia, and Nellie's reading and writing are excellent."

"And I'm leff hammed!" Nellie shouted triumphantly.

"Nellie, for heaven's sake lower your voice," Martha said, casting a glance toward Miss Lyons.

Miss Lyons laughed.

"It's true, though. Nellie is left-handed."

"Why, she's the only one," Ma said. "All the children are right-handed, except . . ." Her voice trailed off suddenly. The table fell quiet. Miss Lyons looked from one face to another.

"Our brother Sammy was left-handed as well," Martha said quietly, picking up a platter of fried onions and apples. "May I serve you seconds, Jennie?"

"Yes, please," she answered, quickly lifting her plate. In that way she had of knowing what to say, and when to say nothing at all, Miss Lyons went on eating. That is a kind of intelligence that you just can't learn, Bill thought. You either got it or you don't. And she's got it.

It had been over a year since Sammy had died, but it was still hard for the family to talk about the oldest Cody boy. Now that Ma was expecting another child, Bill hoped the subject might become less painful. Many was the time he had a memory of Sammy he wanted to share with his family but stopped himself. Maybe after the new baby was born, it would be easier. Bill knew both Ma and Pa were hoping for another boy. He'd listened to them talk when they thought he was asleep. Maybe they could start talking about Sammy if Ma had another son.

Martha had told Bill she was sure the baby was a boy. She could tell, she said, by the shape of Ma's belly. To Bill she didn't look any different than she had when she was expecting Mary Hannah or Nellie. But Martha spoke in that all-knowing way she had, and she wasn't to be talked out of her opinion.

Anyway, Bill hoped she was right. It would be nice to have a brother again.

Martha was clearing away the supper dishes and setting out a pie for dessert when Turk began to bark. Bill was at the door instantly.

"Wait, Bill," Pa said, but Bill had already cracked the door and was peering outside. He could see a rider now, in a blue uniform. The horse was coming fast. Bill gave a surprised exclamation.

"Why, it's Corporal Sam Curtis!" he said.

"Who?" asked Pa, standing behind him in the doorway.

"From Fort Leavenworth. We both met him last summer, remember? The day . . ."

Pa nodded. "I remember. Nice young man. What's he want with us, though?"

Corporal Curtis was tying his horse up. He then headed quickly for the door, which Bill opened all the way to let him in.

"Good to see you, son," Pa said. "We're just about to have some pie. Would you like some?"

Bill wanted to be the one to extend the welcome to Corporal Curtis. But instead of growing irritated, he tried to remember that while Pa was home, he was head of the household again, injured or not. It was only proper that Pa be the one to do the inviting.

"'Preciate it," Corporal Curtis was saying, "but there's no time. I came to give you the heads up.

There's trouble brewing. Group of border ruffians were up at the fort this afternoon, carrying on. I over-heard some of them talking about riding over here tonight and doing some mischief."

Ma gave a little gasp in spite of herself, and Miss Lyons leaped to her feet.

"Shall I stable our horses, Corporal, so it don't look as if there are visitors here?" Bill asked.

Corporal Curtis shook his head.

"I think it might be better if it did look like there were some more folks here. I see you already have a guest. How do you do, ma'am. Sam Curtis is the name."

Only a terrible person could feel jealous at a time like this, but Bill sure didn't like the way Corporal Curtis smiled at Miss Lyons.

"I could put Little Gray and Prince outside as well," Julia said.

"Not Prince, silly," Bill said. "They know him. Stole him last year, don't you remember? He broke free and came back to me the next week," he added for the benefit of Miss Lyons and Sam.

"It'll be too dark for anyone to recognize a horse they stole five months ago," Julia retorted. Bill's face burned, from both anger at Julia for contradicting him in front of everyone and embarrassment that she had a good point.

"I'll see to the horses, Corporal Sam Curtis, and I

am Jennie Lyons," Miss Lyons said, dashing outside.

Sam grinned and looked pleased with himself.

"Sorry not to come for a more neighborly visit," he said, entering the cabin. "Now let's get thinking."

"If they come inside, they'll find out that Pa's here," Bill said. "There's just no place to hide him."

"Then I'd best go out to the cornfields and lay low like I did last time," Pa said.

"You can't, Isaac," Ma said. "It's cold enough tonight for a frost. You'd catch your death out there."

"Ma's right," Bill said, but Pa shook his head.

"Don't see as we have much choice, unless I go straight out and give myself up to them."

Ma gave a cry, and Pa held out his hand to indicate he didn't really mean it. Still, Bill knew that if it came down to protecting his family, Pa would indeed hand himself over to the border ruffians. It was what a courageous man would do.

"The way I see it, the trick is to make them not *want* to come inside," Corporal Curtis said. Bill looked at him anxiously. Bill's mind had gone horribly blank. His normally quick-thinking brain seemed cotton soft and useless.

"How many pairs of boots do you have around here?" Corporal Curtis said, as Miss Lyons came back inside.

"Probably four or five, what with the ones that still fit and ones that are worn through," Bill answered.

"How 'bout men's coats, hats? Work shirts?"

"We got 'em," Bill said. He wanted to ask Corporal Curtis what his plan was, but he knew there wasn't time. Best to follow orders, ask questions later.

"Can you get them collected?" Corporal Curtis asked.

"I'll do it," Julia said quickly. Before anyone could say anything, she was out the door and running for the stable.

"She knows where they all are," Bill said. "We keep the work boots in the stable."

"Good. And whatever firearms you have, now would be a good time to load them."

Pa fetched his shotgun, moving quicker than Bill had seen him do in a long time. They had another old rifle that didn't work but looked as though it might, and Corporal Curtis himself had a government-issue Colt Army pistol, polished until it gleamed.

Julia came in with three pairs of old boots, and Martha fetched two more from the bedroom, along with Pa's shirts and jackets. They piled everything on the floor.

"This is all we have," Julia said.

"That'll do," Corporal Curtis said.

"What are you thinking, son?" asked Pa. Bill wished he'd stop calling Corporal Curtis that.

"Well, it's dark out, and these men will probably have a few drinks in them when they get here. Even sober they probably aren't the smartest folks in the Territory. We know it's just us and we only have two guns between us, but they don't have to know that. It's how we act and sound that counts. Works in the dragoons all the time."

"You mean we're going to create the impression that there are other men from the fort here?" asked Miss Lyons.

Corporal Curtis rewarded her with a wide smile.

"That's right, ma'am. That's exactly right. We could start, Mrs. Cody, by getting every candle and lantern you have lit and near the window."

Ma nodded, and she and Martha began to help them.

"And then we could get some of your sisters into these boots," Corporal Curtis said.

"Why?" Bill asked, already starting to help Eliza Alice into a pair of huge worn boots twice as big as her feet.

"Because, *silly*, the more clomping around there is, the more big folks it will seem are here," Julia said.

That was twice she'd humiliated him in front of Miss Lyons, and Pa, and Corporal Curtis! If they got through this night, Bill swore to himself, he'd fill her bed with frogs and centipedes.

Eliza Alice was grimacing slightly, but she obediently laced the boots as tight as she could while Bill got Nellie into a pair.

"Dirty boots!" Nellie exclaimed, laughing. This

isn't a game, Bill wanted to say. But maybe it was better she did think it a game. Why tell her their performance was of deadly importance?

"Now for the overcoats and hats," Sam said. "Those are for Mrs. Cody, Miss Cody, and Miss Lyons—that is, if you don't mind doing some acting this evening."

"I believe I can manage that," Martha replied, a little crisply. Maybe Bill wasn't the only one who didn't like the way Corporal Curtis smiled at Miss Lyons.

Ma finished lighting the lanterns and candles, and Pa was loading his shotgun. Eliza Alice, Nellie, and Julia were all wearing old work boots. Bill had his own on already. Ma, Martha, and Miss Lyons now all wore large jackets or shirts, and men's hats, their hair tucked underneath.

"I feel like Kit Carson," Miss Lyons said. Bill felt proud to know Miss Lyons, thinking to mention his old hero at that moment.

Bill looked out the door. "No sign of them," he said.

"Turk will bark before we can see them," Pa said.

Bill knew Pa was right, but his face flushed. It was bad enough having Julia taunting him, but was Pa to criticize him too? He was used to being in charge. Ever since Pa had left, back in the fall, Bill had been the man of the family. He hadn't always liked it, and often worried he wouldn't be up to the job.

But he did it. Now Pa was back, and finally growing stronger. And Corporal Curtis was here, and he seemed to know exactly what to do. Pa and Corporal Curtis were actual grown men, after all. No matter how much he did, how many good ideas he had, and how hard he worked, Bill was still a boy. Not even into the two-number ages yet. Where was his place now?

He stood in the corner, chewing over his thoughts. They were ready for whatever was coming, but the night was quiet. The younger girls sat around the table. Julia had the dozing Mary Hannah in her arms. Bill thought Eliza Alice looked funny, sitting primly in the enormous boots as she worked a needle and thread through her mending. But he didn't laugh. The silence outside seemed worse than the sound of any drunken gang. It was the waiting and the anticipation that were the most difficult to take.

Turk began to growl. Julia jumped, and Corporal Curtis gestured for everyone to be silent. Miss Lyons set her jaw in a determined way and pulled Pa's old hat down around her ears.

Corporal Curtis was listening intently, his head cocked to one side.

"Aren't you going to go look?" Bill whispered.

Corporal Curtis shook his head. "Wouldn't look right," he whispered back. "The idea is we don't care if there's anyone outside or not, 'cause we got nothing to fear."

Bill whistled to Turk, and the dog, his hackles raised, reluctantly trotted over to his master. Bill kept one hand firmly on his collar and watched Corporal Curtis listening.

There were definitely people outside. Bill could hear muffled voices, and the occasional unfamiliar whinny of a strange horse. He was almost exploding inside, knowing the border ruffians were so close and yet doing nothing but standing with his hand on his dog's collar.

"All right," Corporal Curtis said suddenly. He picked up his long pistol.

"Miss Lyons, if you'd come stand behind me in the doorway, back a few feet," he said. She nodded.

"Mr. Cody, why don't you take the shotgun and stand by the window," Sam said.

"I'll do that," Bill said, reaching for Pa's gun. Corporal Curtis didn't know how weak Pa had been.

"I'll do it," Pa said, taking the gun from Bill. "It's my gun and I'm not straight-out helpless, thank you." He didn't even glance at Bill as he went to the door.

"All right, then, Bill, you're in charge of noise-making," said Corporal Curtis, before Bill could even think about what Pa had just said. "I need you and your sisters walking around, moving chairs, opening drawers. Nothing too wild, just a constant sort of ruckus."

He was being stuck with the *girls*? After months of being the man of his house, he not only felt like a child again, he was starting to get *treated* like one. But all he said was "All right."

"Then here we go," Corporal Curtis replied. He had the brightest lantern, which he put on the table. Pa, Ma, and Martha stood in front of the lamp. Seen through the window, they should only look like the silhouettes of men, lit from behind. Pa stuck the barrel of his shotgun out the window. Corporal Curtis walked over to the door while Miss Lyons in her man's overcoat stood behind him. Straightening his corporal's cap and giving a tug to his neat blue uniform, he opened the door and pointed his pistol.

"You out there," he called in a booming voice. There was no reply.

"Ain't no use pretending—we seen you," Corporal Curtis said. He had dropped his Massachusetts accent and proper speech. He sounded more like Pa now.

"Who's talkin'?" came a voice from the dark. It was Charlie Dunn, Bill knew instantly.

"Lieutenant Curtis of the Second Dragoons, you scoundrel. You best take your people home, before I send my men out after you!"

Bill cast a glance at Corporal Curtis leaning against the doorway, his pistol pointing out, and Miss Lyons standing straight as a poker behind him, looking for all the world like a wiry young man.

"We got business with the abolitionist cuss," called Dunn. "We don't aim to make no trouble with you."

"Why, you insolent puke!" cried Corporal Curtis,

leaning farther out the door. "You'd best think twice before you pick a fight with the dragoons. My men and I are having a peaceable conference here with Jim Lane, and you'd best let us continue. If I hear one more 'abolitionist cuss' out of you, I'm gonna start me a gunfight!"

There was a brief silence. Bill heard the name Lane being repeated outside. Lane was a hotheaded member of the antislavery Free Soil party. He had a reputation for violence and was widely feared.

"Where's Lane?" Dunn called. "That him behind you? Tell him to show himself!"

Corporal Curtis made an explosive noise of rage.

"Why, you rascally horse thief, I ain't got another ounce of patience!" Corporal Curtis turned inside and shouted toward Bill and the girls.

"Private Lewis! Private Simpson! Corporal Smith! Draw your weapons and outside on the double! I want those men rounded up and tied tight."

He turned back toward the doorway.

"We'll see how insolent you all are after a few weeks in the Leavenworth jail!" Corporal Curtis shouted. Bill gestured to his sisters, and the night was suddenly filled with the sounds of chairs scraping back on the floor and heavy boots thudding on wood.

"Come on, boys, pack it up," called Dunn's voice suddenly. Moments later the sound of four or five horses galloping off echoed through the darkness. Within minutes, the night had fallen silent once again.

No one spoke. Eliza unlaced her boots. Still standing near the window, Ma began to unbutton Pa's old coat. Bill noticed her hands were shaking. She said nothing. There was nothing to be said.

In the morning the sun came up as usual. But examining the dirt outside the door, Bill could see the prints of men's feet and horses all around the cabin.

It was a disturbing sight. But not half so disturbing as the abandoned powder keg in the front yard, and the partly laid fuse that led into the Codys' root cellar.

CHAPTER NINE
A NEW ARRIVAL

★ ★ ★

Two days after Charlie Dunn came to the Codys' cabin, Pa packed his things up and made ready to return to Grasshopper Falls.

"I don't like you traveling alone, Isaac," Ma quietly pleaded. "And you still haven't all your strength back. Wait another week."

Pa shook his head.

"We both know it's high time I was gone," Pa said. "I'm much better now, and Dunn and his men are just watching too close. We got lucky the other night. But if I don't leave, they could catch me next time. And we got a baby on the way."

Bill was sitting in the corner, polishing his saddle. He said nothing, just watched his parents. He'd felt strange ever since Pa had been home. Like something had changed, but he couldn't put his finger on it. First he'd resented Pa's being home but not able to help with the farm, or even talk. Then he'd grown angry at Pa. And after a while he wasn't really angry anymore. But every time he thought he might have things figured out, something else changed.

"I don't know what we'll do without you, Pa," Bill found himself saying suddenly.

"Sure you do," Pa said, and Bill felt alarmed, as if Pa were about to light into him. But then Pa gave him a tired smile. "Sure you do," he repeated. "Don't you see, Bill? It's the only reason I *can* leave. Knowing you're here, and how you'll do without me."

And then Bill really didn't want Pa to go. He was so, so tired. He needed to have free time again. He needed to be with Prince. He needed a friend like Joe Barnes. And most of all he needed his pa. But he said none of these things. Instead, he went out to the stable and got Pa's horse ready.

Pa looked bigger, more like his old self, sitting up tall in Little Gray's saddle. His few things were tucked away in a saddlebag, along with some of Ma's cooking. Ma looked especially tired today, as if she were having trouble catching her breath. Nellie wept bitterly. Eliza Alice hadn't even come outside.

They couldn't even count down the days until Pa would come home again. As before, Pa just didn't know when it would be safe for him to come back to Salt Creek. If it would ever be safe again.

Bill felt Julia watching him. She'd been doing that a lot lately, but she'd long since stopped asking what was wrong, or trying to get him to talk. Bill knew he should be happy about that. Wasn't that what he'd wanted all along, for Julia to just stop pestering him? After all, he could never be honest with her. She was his sister. The whole family had been depending on him, and they would all do so again with Pa gone. He could not tell any of them, least of all Julia, of how tired it made him feel. And how scared.

Bill knew he couldn't tell a person something like that and then expect her to trust him to keep the family safe. If Pa knew, he wouldn't go back to the safety of Grasshopper Falls. If Julia knew, she wouldn't sleep at night. If Ma knew . . . No, no one must know. So he kept it all to himself, wound tightly inside him like rope around his innards.

Ma reached up and took Pa's hand as he sat in the saddle, giving it one last squeeze. Her other hand rested protectively on her belly. She stood there a moment, then stepped away. Pa gave the horse a nudge with his knees and set off, heading west. He did not look back. Bill didn't blame him. He remembered the Bible story Ma had read about Lot's wife looking back and turning into a pillar of salt. A person should always look straight ahead. Anything else was not good sense.

Enough standing still, Bill thought. There were chores to be done. The cow wasn't going to milk herself, nor was the corn going to get hoed unless Bill did it. He mumbled something about the day not getting any younger and headed for the stable.

"Bill idn't any fun no more," he heard Nellie say. He kept walking without making a retort. Nellie was right, of course. He wasn't fun anymore. He didn't have the time for it. Somebody had to muck out the stalls, right?

Prince turned his head and looked at Bill as he closed the stable door behind him. Bill felt a stab of guilt. How long had it been since he'd given Prince an extra rubdown? Smuggled him a carrot? Maybe after dinner he could make a little time. He patted Prince twice on the back, then grabbed the pitchfork and started shoveling the old hay and manure out of the horse's stall. He worked quickly, going from one stall to the next. Then he pitched fresh hay under the horses' feet.

There was a bridle needing mending, and Bill thought he might as well do that while he remembered. He'd just found a comfortable place to sit and work when the stable door opened and Eliza Alice came in. Bill raised his eyebrows. Eliza Alice never came into the stable.

"Martha says come inside quick as you can," she said. Bill climbed to his feet. There was no point in asking Eliza Alice anything. She would merely repeat Martha's orders. Bill took his little sister's hand and let her lead him back to the cabin.

"Martha," Bill called out as he stepped over the threshold, "I'm here, but I really ain't got time to spare right now. Martha?"

Julia came out of Ma's bedroom holding Mary Hannah on one hip and beckoned to Bill.

"Can't anybody talk?" Bill asked crossly, following Julia into Ma's bedroom. He stopped short in the doorway. Ma was sitting on the edge of her bed breathing heavily, both hands on her heavy belly. Martha was sitting behind her, pressing her fists into Ma's lower back. She glanced up at Bill.

"Baby's coming," she said. "We'll need to get a fire going and put the kettle on, and someone will need to go for Doc Hathaway."

"Ma?" Bill asked nervously. She gave him a tight smile.

"It's okay, Bill," she said. "Everything's fine."

"It just seems so fast," Bill stammered.

"She was laboring all morning," Martha said. "Just didn't want to worry Pa before he set out."

"Eliza Alice is taking Nellie and Mary Hannah

to pick some berries," Julia said. "I'll go for Doc Hathaway, Bill, if you'll get the fire started for the kettle."

"I'll go for Doc," Bill said quickly. He could plant corn and tend animals and even put out a fire if need be. But Bill knew he would be useless here in the cabin. Helping bring a baby into the world was one skill Bill felt pretty sure he didn't have. And he couldn't think of anything worse than sticking around when he couldn't be useful.

"There's time yet," Ma said.

"All the same, I'd best get going," Bill said. He hesitated a moment.

"Martha?" he asked. "That okay?"

It didn't feel right, leaving while this was going on. But in the matter of baby delivering Martha was far and away the most eligible for command.

"Yes," she replied. "Just let Doc Hathaway know the baby probably won't be coming till around suppertime."

"Right," Bill said, beating a hasty retreat as Ma bent forward with a low moan.

He half ran back to the stable.

"Come on, Prince," he said to his horse, grabbing the tack and swinging open the door to the stall.

"Told you I'd take you for a ride later, didn't I? We gotta go fetch Doc Hathaway."

Prince looked about as pleased as a horse ever had to be saddled up. Bill felt in control again on

Prince's back, unlike the helpless boy he seemed to be standing back in Ma's room.

The ride to Doc Hathaway's took only about ten or fifteen minutes, even at a relaxed pace. The house looked as big and comfortable as ever. Doc had added clapboards and painted them a fresh, lively yellow. Not for the first time Bill wondered why Doc bothered to farm at all. He always seemed to have plenty of money, family money as Pa called it, and his medical services were always in demand.

But he wasn't here to figure out Doc's life. Bill dismounted and tied Prince to the fence rail. He knocked on the front door. When Miss Lyons opened it, Bill immediately turned red.

"Why Bill Cody," she said, brushing a curl off her forehead. "If this isn't a nice surprise."

"Ma'am," Bill said, looking at his feet. It hadn't occurred to him his teacher would answer the door. Was he going to have to explain about the baby to her? He didn't think he'd be able to do it.

"I Doc for the . . . I Doc . . . is the doc . . . ?"

It was the best he could do.

"Doctor and Mrs. Hathaway both rode down to Fort Leavenworth this morning," said Miss Lyons, with her usual genius of understanding the incomprehensible. "One of the officers' wives was in her confinement and thought her time was coming this afternoon. Is everything all right?"

Bill stared. He couldn't get any more words out,

not even wrong ones. How was he supposed to say the word *labor* to Miss Lyons?

"Oh, Bill," she said, opening the door wider. "Is it your ma's time too?"

Bill nodded, almost sick with relief.

She was all action, already moving.

"I'll leave a note for the doc," she said. "And I'll come back with you myself."

Bill wanted to tell her that wasn't necessary, but he was afraid she'd believe him.

"Would you saddle up Bonnie for me?" she called from the kitchen. "Her tack is hanging just outside her stall."

"Yes, ma'am," Bill said. He went out the front door and headed around back to the Hathaway stable. The doc had four fine horses of his own, and the fifth stall was occupied by Bonnie.

As Bill lifted the saddle, the horse turned her head and looked at him. Bill looked back at her and noticed with surprise that her eyes were perfect, jewellike spheres. Bill and Bonnie stared at each other for a moment; then Bill resumed tacking up, gently placing the saddle over her bumpy, flea-bitten back.

A few minutes later, when Miss Lyons asked Bill if he didn't think Bonnie was a beautiful creature, Bill looked his teacher straight in the eye and said yes.

Bill had never known the time to pass so slowly. It seemed like days since Miss Lyons had gone inside to help Martha deliver Ma's baby. Bill had done every chore he could think of, hoeing the corn twice, washing all the tack with saddle soap, mending the bridle, and fixing the ox yoke where the wood was beginning to split.

The trick was to find more chores that he could get done without going too far away from the cabin, and also without going too close. Inside was completely out of the question. Eliza Alice had set up some chairs outside and was helping Nellie stitch her sampler while Mary Hannah watched. Julia was flitting around like a hummingbird, running to the creek to fetch more water, checking on the girls, going inside, and coming back outside to tell everyone there was nothing yet to tell.

He was entirely useless, Bill told himself. His presence was absolutely no good to Ma or to anyone. All he wanted to do was curl up somewhere and fall asleep. It seemed that the kind of tired that came from not being able to do anything was much worse than the kind that came from having to do everything.

The cabin door opened and Julia came outside holding a plate of bread and cold sliced ham.

"This will have to do for supper," she said. "Eliza Alice, I'll take the sewing inside so it doesn't get mussed."

"I'll do it," Eliza Alice said, gathering the sampler, thread, and needle into her little sewing basket. She stood looking at the cabin for a moment.

"Ma will be fine," Julia said to her younger sister. "It just takes a long time sometimes."

Eliza Alice didn't respond, but she snapped the lid closed on her sewing basket and headed inside.

"She's getting odd. Don't you think she's getting odd?" Julia asked Bill quietly, as Nellie retied the sash around Mary Hannah's dress. Bill had gotten so used to Julia giving him the cold shoulder, it took him a moment to realize she was talking to him.

"Eliza Alice? I think she's the same as she ever was. Kind of comforting, actually. The only thing that don't ever change around here is Eliza Alice and her quiet, indoor ways."

"I suppose," Julia said, breaking the bread into pieces. "I ought to spend more time with her, I expect." She popped a piece of bread into her mouth, then burst out, "It's taking so much longer for the baby to come this time! I remember with Mary Hannah the whole thing wasn't six hours from start to finish. And Ma said it took even less time with Nellie."

"If Pa had known, he would have stayed," Bill said, a little defensively.

"No, it's best he isn't here. Men just get in the way during a birth. Sorry," she added quickly. "I didn't mean you."

Bill shrugged it off, but it hurt. He was in the way. A sore thumb, no good to anyone.

"It'll be dark soon," Julia said, as Eliza Alice came back outside. "We'll have to go in before long. Mary

Hannah will catch a cold."

"Could we go to the stable?" Bill asked, as Julia made a little sandwich and handed it to Nellie.

"Hamwich!" Nellie said, taking a huge bite.

"It'll be practically as cold in the stable as out here," Julia replied.

"Well, what do you want me to do, Julia, build another cabin?" Bill snapped.

Instead of returning his retort, Julia's face crumpled, and she began to cry.

"Wha . . . I didn't . . ." Bill stammered.

"Why is Julia crying?" asked Nellie with her mouth full.

"I'm not crying!" Julia said, wiping her eyes. She turned away from Nellie and shot Bill a sideways look.

"I'm just scared, Bill," she whispered. "What if Ma isn't all right? What if something happens? Aren't you scared? Don't you ever get scared?"

It was the perfect time to tell her just how scared he got, how he was chased by his fears into sleep every night. Could he admit this to Julia, could he tell her how weak he really was inside?

The question in his mind was interrupted by the high sound of a baby's cries piercing the sky. Almost immediately, Miss Lyons came outside. She was smiling.

"It's a boy," she said.

CHAPTER TEN

ABOLITION SCHOOL

★　　★　　★

M a wrote his name in the family Bible, right below Mary Hannah's. Charles Whitney Cody, May 10, 1855. Finally, Bill had a little brother and Ma and Pa a new son.

Bill loved the little baby the second he set eyes on him. He had a scrunched, peanutlike face blotched with red places, but Bill could see straightaway he looked like a Cody top to bottom.

"He's making a mad face," Nellie said. "Like Bill's mad face. Why?"

Martha had given the children precisely five minutes with Ma before they were to make themselves scarce and bunk down with Bill. They were gathered around the bed, where Ma lay cuddling the newborn in her arms. It was after ten o'clock now, and Martha slipped into the kitchen, where Miss Lyons was making some tea.

"I don't have a mad face," Bill said.

"Yes, you do," said Julia and Nellie at the same time. Even Eliza Alice laughed.

"All newborns have tight little faces the first day or two," Ma explained, rubbing Charles on his tiny back. "He'll start looking more like his baby self in a few days."

"Can I touch him?" Nellie asked, wide-eyed.

"Don't touch the top of his head," Eliza Alice said. "It's too soft still. Touch his feet instead."

Bill and Julia both stared at Eliza Alice, surprised.

"How did you know that?" asked Julia.

"I remember from Mary Hannah," Eliza Alice explained. "I remember the doctor showing us the little soft place, and promising not to touch it so I wouldn't hurt the baby. I expect Charles would have the same place on his head."

It was about the longest speech Bill could recall Eliza Alice ever making. Maybe Julia was right about Eliza Alice being different.

"Your memory is better than mine," Julia said. Eliza Alice smiled.

"That's enough now," said Martha from the

doorway. "Let Ma have her rest while the baby is still sleeping."

Martha made an excellent boss, Bill thought.

"Jennie is going to spend the night. She says there will be school tomorrow," Martha continued. "Ma's exhausted, and it will be best to have you all out of the cabin."

Not, of course, including Martha, Bill thought. With her take-charge ways, Bill knew she actually would be a great help to Ma these first difficult days after Charles's birth. He'd be more than happy to go to school. Anyway, the corn was in the ground, and it wasn't yet time to plant the wheat. Bill didn't want to fall behind on his writing and penmanship.

It was crowded up in the loft, with Julia, Eliza Alice, and Nellie all sleeping there with him. Their breathing was loud in the darkness. Julia snored a little. Within minutes Bill knew he was the only one still awake. He was surprised at the amount of noise three sleeping sisters could make. Was it just a few months ago he'd actually missed having company up there in the loft?

Baby Charles was a great blessing, an innocent miracle who had appeared in Kansas Territory during a difficult time. But Bill couldn't help thinking that now there was yet another Cody for him to help care for, worry about, and protect. What if the baby took sick? Or what if Ma did?

Thoughts flew in and out of Bill's mind like a

swarm of flies. More crops should be planted. Maybe an additional field should get plowed. Would the summer bring enough rain to keep the crops healthy? What if the locusts came this year? Or a drought? Where would the money come from if they had no crops to sell?

At dawn, just as his sisters were beginning to stir and stretch beside him, Bill was still wide-awake, alone with his thoughts.

Miss Lyons slowed her pace enough to let Julia, Nellie, and Eliza Alice run slightly ahead. It was a spectacular spring morning. The sky was a rich, cool blue, and the landscape glimmered a vibrant green. The air was thick with the sweet smell of soil and grass and new growth. Things began again in the spring. Life gave the world a second chance.

But Bill could not enjoy the morning. His head felt heavy and swollen, his eyes little slits. He was awake when he was supposed to be sleeping, and sleepy when he was meant to be awake. He noticed Miss Lyons looking at him. He was too tired even to blush.

"Bill, are you feeling ill?" she asked. "You look even more tired today than usual."

"I'm all right," Bill said automatically. "Just slept funny. We saw Pa off in the morning, and then with the baby coming, it was hard to sleep right."

They walked in silence for a few moments. Then Miss Lyons changed the subject.

"It must have been difficult having your pa home when he was feeling so ill. I expect you had all the worry of helping care for him, but none of the benefit of his advice, since he was too ill to give it."

Bill almost stopped in his tracks. How did she *do* that? Was there anything about him Miss Lyons *didn't* know? Bill coughed to hide his embarrassment.

"It's funny to think back on it now, but I was actually quite nervous about coming here to teach," Miss Lyons said.

"You were?" Bill asked. Miss Lyons just didn't seem to be the nervous type.

"I wasn't sure what would be asked of me," Miss Lyons said. "And I knew whatever it was, I'd be expected to measure up. Alone, living with strange folks. I had my doubts, believe me. I was so relieved to find how kind and good you all were, and to meet Martha."

"Martha?" Bill asked. He knew Martha and Miss Lyons spent much of their free time together, but he had never really wondered why.

"I can talk to Martha," Miss Lyons said. "We're about the same age, similar families. She understands me. And once I knew that I had one person in all of Kansas Territory that I could talk honestly to, I knew I had nothing to fear."

"I had a friend like that, back in Iowa," Bill said. "Name was Joe Barnes. We played together all the time, told each other everything. But there's no Joe in Kansas."

Miss Lyons nodded. "And writing letters just isn't the same," she said. "Joe isn't here. He can't really understand your new life the way he could your old one."

"That's right," Bill said.

"Well, you must look for a new friend, Bill," Miss Lyons said.

"Where?" Bill asked, gesturing at the vast, empty landscape.

"I find it's always best to start in your own backyard," she said, smiling.

There was nothing in Bill's backyard but a couple of hens. But he appreciated the way Miss Lyons was talking to him. Like he was as grown up as Martha. That alone made him feel better.

"Anyway," Bill said, "even if Joe Barnes was here, there isn't any time to play the way we used to."

"Life has a funny way of evening out," Miss Lyons said. "You're missing out on a lot of playing this year. But someday it will come back to you."

"I'll probably be grown before that happens," Bill said.

"Maybe," Miss Lyons replied. "But grown-ups like to play just as much as children do, I can assure you. And in the meantime, Bill, don't lose faith. You are never given more than you can bear."

"That's what scares me," Bill said. "Getting more and more to bear, with nothing ever changing. After Charlie Dunn come by the other night, I think we all realized it won't be safe for Pa here for a long, long time. Maybe never. I can't count on him coming home no more."

"Anymore," Miss Lyons corrected gently. "Haven't you ever heard your ma say that when God closes a door, somewhere else He opens a window?" Miss Lyons asked. Bill nodded, watching Nellie and Julia skipping down the road ahead of them, as Eliza Alice trailed more soberly behind.

"Well, sometimes you have to let the door close first, and have faith that the window will open. Do you understand?"

"I don't think so, ma'am," Bill said.

"You have to ask for help even though you don't think any will come."

"Ask who?" Bill asked, feeling dumber by the minute.

"Anyone. God. Your family. Yourself. Just say it out loud. I need help."

Bill looked at his teacher.

"I need help," he said at last. She smiled, satisfied.

"It will come," she replied.

Down the road, Nellie and Julia had stopped skipping and were standing perfectly still. A moment later, Bill saw what they were looking at, and began to run.

The schoolhouse shanty was half burned, the wood still smoking and falling in on itself. The blackboard had been pulled off and sat propped outside. On it, etched in crude letters, were the words NO MOR ABLISHIN SCHUL.

"Well," said Miss Lyons. "This does present a problem."

Once again, Bill thought, Miss Lyons had it right.

CHAPTER ELEVEN
PARTING COMPANY

The girls had tidied for two hours in anticipation of the Hathaways' arrival. They'd set out the good china, and Julia had baked a cake. They couldn't wait to show off Charles to their neighbors, and to Miss Lyons, who hadn't seen him since he was a newborn four whole days ago.

But now the merry gathering had fallen abruptly silent. Everyone was staring at Doc in disbelief. Finally, Bill spoke up.

"Moving?" he asked. "Where? Why?"

"Back to New York," Doc replied. "When my brother went back east to fetch his family here, they stopped in New York. Ended up staying, and now they've asked me to move back. Got me an offer to join a practice. I'll never make a go of this farming thing, and with Kansas Territory getting hotter by the minute, I just can't see staying here."

"I don't understand," Ma said. "Addie, you never said anything about it."

"Let's just say things have changed for me in the last month," Mrs. Hathaway said, nodding toward Charles.

So Mrs. Hathaway was expecting too. And that was enough to make them move?

"Your young'un would have a friend almost his age," Bill said hopefully. But he could tell what she was thinking. She doesn't want to raise a child in a place where Americans are attacking other Americans over a vote. She doesn't think it is going to get safer.

"We hate to leave you," Doc said. "God knows we do. We thought and thought about it. I know better than anyone your situation. But it's different for me. I'm a city man, not a farmer. I don't know why I ever got myself into this. And with the election, the Territorial Legislature is already showing its true colors."

"What do you mean?" asked Ma.

"Well, they issued a slave code, making it punishable by death to help a slave revolt or escape, even if it's just through an article you write for the paper. And it says they're entitled to put a man in jail just for giving an opinion against slavery that might lead to a slave's escaping. That means they can put anyone in prison with the flimsiest excuse, and there isn't a thing anyone can do about it. I just can't see risking it, not with my farm failing, a job waiting for me back east, and a child on the way."

"Can't President Pierce stop them?" Bill asked.

"I don't know, Bill," said Doc Hathaway, sounding tired. "He's doing what he can. I hear he's replacing Governor Reeder with a new man. But he's already shown he's not going to come out against these folks outright. He's got his own reputation to take care of, I guess."

"What about you, Jennie?" Martha asked. "Where will you go?"

Bill's heart gave a jump as it occurred to him that perhaps she would move in with them. But he was quickly disappointed.

"I'll be moving to Leavenworth City," she said.

"Leavenworth?" Bill asked. Miss Lyons nodded.

"That was a pretty clear message we got from the border ruffians the other day," she said. "The school is ruined, and they don't want me teaching here. Now is simply not the time to take a stand. I don't like it, but I'm sensible enough to know that as many schools as we build in Salt Creek, they'll just come and burn them down. Next time we might all be inside when they try. It doesn't make sense for you all to put yourselves in danger that way."

"So you're moving to Leavenworth?" Martha asked. "Does this mean you've heard from Mr. Hook?"

Miss Lyons smiled, and her face flushed.

"Yes I have, Martha," she said. She looked around at the children.

"Mr. Hook is a young man I knew back in Ohio. He's done well for himself now, and he feels settled enough to take a wife."

"Who's he going to marry?" asked Bill. Miss Lyons and Martha laughed.

"Why, Jennie, of course," Martha said. Bill's stomach turned to lead.

"Leavenworth is really quite close," Miss Lyons said quickly. "I'll be able to visit, and I want you all to visit me too. Perhaps some of you will decide to take some schooling there. Once we're settled in a house, we'll have room for you to stay."

"That's a lovely offer," Ma said. "We'll need Bill here of course, but perhaps we could arrange for Julia to take some schooling in the fall."

Julia? Why Julia? Bill wanted to shout. She would get to go off and live with Miss Lyons in the city. He would be stuck back on the farm with the corn and the leaky roof and the stable that needed rebuilding. When would it ever be *his* chance?

Before he could even think about what he was doing, Bill had pushed his chair back with a scrape, flung open the front door, and run outside in the direction of the cornfield. He ran until his lungs felt like they would burst, then threw himself on the grass and began to sob with frustration and rage and exhaustion.

He didn't know who he was anymore. He had no friend. He had no one to talk to. Now even Miss Lyons, who had talked to him like a grown-up, was leaving him behind. Where was this window God was supposed to open?

He wept until he felt sick. Then at last he stopped. He rolled over onto his back and stared at the sky, wiping his eyes and his nose with the sleeve of his shirt. At least no one had followed him and caught him crying like a little girl whose dolly had gotten busted.

There were tiny puffs of clouds far overhead. They looked like billowy sheep grazing in a blue pasture. Bill watched them, slowing his breathing until he began to feel more normal. He took comfort in the presence of the sky. It arched over him in its protective expanse, no matter what he felt or did. It was the same sky that Pa saw in Grasshopper Falls, and that Joe saw back in Iowa. It was everybody's sky, and in sharing it he felt a little closer to the people he'd left behind, or who'd left him.

After a long time, Bill sat up and looked back toward the cabin in the distance. They were all still inside, thinking and saying heaven knew what about him. He ought to get back. He'd wasted enough time eating cake and watching the Hathaways admiring his baby brother. There was more work to be done.

Bill hoped Miss Lyons was right when she said that life had a way of evening out, and that the playful times he had given up now would someday come back to him. He got to his feet and took one last look up at the friendly sky.

"I need help," he told it. Then he turned and headed back home.

It was as if his outburst had never happened. The Hathaways and Miss Lyons said their good-byes and promised to let the Codys know when a moving date was set. Julia and Eliza Alice set out to get some kindling for the fireplace, and Ma gathered the yawning Charles in her arms. On her way to the bedroom, she paused by Bill, who was pulling on his work boots.

"Bill?" she asked softly. "Is there something you want to talk about?"

"No, ma'am," he said, glancing up at her to avoid being rude.

"I know how much you enjoyed school," she said. "It breaks my heart to have you stop."

"I know that," Bill said. "It's only school. I only acted like I enjoyed it to— Well, it don't make much difference to me." Ma hesitated, searching Bill's face.

Charles began to fuss, making the unhappy squeaking noises that generally came right before real crying. Ma shifted him to her other shoulder and rubbed his little back. She sighed.

"Your time will come, Bill," she said. "I promise you. Someday, your time will come."

"I know," Bill said quietly. "Baby's getting cranky."

"I'll go put him in his cradle," Ma said. "I guess it's time we wrote to Elijah again, let him know Pa's been and gone, and that the Hathaways are moving. Will you ask Julia to write when she comes back?"

"I can do it," Bill said.

"Don't bother yourself," Ma said. "Julia will have it done quick as a flash."

"I can do it," Bill repeated, bristling. "You ain't seen my handwriting since . . . You haven't seen my handwriting, I mean. Miss Lyons said I showed remarkable improvement."

"Oh, Bill," Ma said. "So much has changed about you I haven't had time to see. Of course you may write the letter to Elijah. Can you take it down to Fort Leavenworth tomorrow?"

Bill nodded, more than happy to spend his morning on horseback and see the sights at the fort.

Long after the supper dishes had been cleared, Bill sat at the table with a slate and pencil. He wrote each word with painstaking slowness, his tongue tucked into the corner of his mouth and his brow furrowed with concentration. It wasn't enough that it look good. Bill wanted it to be perfect.

As he prepared to leave the fort after delivering the letter, Bill heard someone call out to him.

"Why, Bill Cody, as I live and breathe!"

Bill stopped Prince short and turned around, expecting to see Corporal Curtis. His mouth dropped open, and the air went right out of his lungs and left him speechless.

Horace Billings was standing there, plain as you please, grinning his horse-wrangling grin.

"Horace!" yelled Bill, leaping down out of the saddle. He almost rushed right into Horace's arms before he remembered that this might not be the manly thing to do. So he skidded to a stop just in front of Horace and breathed an excited "Hey!"

Horace laughed.

"Hey yourself," he said. "And lookie here. Is this the same Prince I green broke for you last summer? He's looking mighty fine."

Bill swelled with pride. The days he'd spent watching Horace break Prince had been among the very happiest of his life. The last thing he'd expected was to see Horace now. When he'd ridden off last summer, he'd been vague as to where he was going, and when he'd be back. But he was here now, and that was all that mattered.

"Been out west rounding up wild horses for the

government with some buddies," Horace said. "Quartermaster here's paying me ten dollars for each one! Hoped to stop by and visit your claim if there was time. How's your folks?"

"Ma just had a baby boy," Bill said.

"Ain't that swell," Horace said, unconvincingly. "And your pa?"

Bill swallowed.

"I guess you didn't hear," he said.

"Hear?" Horace asked.

"He got stabbed last September outside Rively's. By a proslavery fella named Charlie Dunn."

Horace whistled. "He okay now?"

"Better than he was," Bill replied. "He's been working over in Grasshopper Falls, running a mill and helping folks lay claims. He means to come back home when things are calmer. But they never seem to get calmer."

"If that don't beat all," Horace said. "If I'da had any idea, I'd have come back east sooner. Did you give up the claim?"

"No, we're still there," said Bill.

"Who's doing the farming?"

"Couple a hired men come over from the neighbor's sometimes. The rest I do, what I can anyway."

"You?" Horace said. "You're taking care of things?"

The way he said it was not insulting but admiring. But Bill only knew how many things didn't get done.

"I do what I can," Bill repeated.

Horace shook his head in amazement.

"I'll be darned. I'll tell you what, then. I'm gonna see about getting my payment from the quartermaster, and maybe look up some of my old buddies. Then I'll ride on over to see your work for myself, maybe visit a spell before I push on. That sound good?"

"Sure thing," Bill said. A lump was rising in his throat. Naturally Horace would be pushing on. A man like Horace always had something on the horizon to make for.

"Good enough," Horace said. He turned and started walking in the direction of the quartermaster's depot. Bill could not have felt more pain if he'd taken an arrow through the heart.

He had longed to see Horace, and his wish had come true. But Horace would not be staying, and it might be years before Bill set eyes on him again. Bill didn't think he could bear it. He felt overwhelmingly lonely. Then a thought came to him. What if Horace was the opening window Miss Lyons had talked about?

"Horace!" Bill called out suddenly.

Horace turned around.

"Horace," Bill called again, walking quickly toward him.

He took a deep breath as he reached his cousin.

"Horace," he said. "I need help."

CHAPTER TWELVE
AN OPEN WINDOW

★   ★   ★

It was as if he'd had a ball and chain around his ankles for the last six months, and suddenly he'd taken his first steps without them, Bill thought. The day still held the same endless list of chores, but now they no longer seemed to be squashing the breath out of him. There was no Miss Lyons to make combing his hair worth it, but Bill polished Prince's saddle until it gleamed before showing it to Horace.

Horace had elected to bunk in the stable, probably to Ma's secret relief. He'd explained he just wasn't used to sleeping in a house, let alone one filled with young'uns, and the sound and smell of the horses would make him feel at home. Besides, he said, whatever was good enough for Rogue, his horse, was good enough for him. But he'd be more than happy to come inside for Ma's cooking.

Horace knew more than any man alive about horses. But he knew less than even Doc Hathaway about farming. So Bill found himself in the peculiar position of explaining what they needed to accomplish, what crops would be planted next, what needed to be tended, when they could expect to begin harvesting. Horace listened patiently, though he often looked bored.

"Don't worry," Horace had told him. "Just 'cause I don't think farming is the most exciting thing I ever done don't mean I can't get the job finished. I done all kinds of work in my day. I said I'd stay through harvest time, and I aim to keep my promise."

After just a few days it seemed as if Horace had always been with them, so naturally did he do the work around the claim.

Ma had not taken to Horace before. He was a horse wrangler, wild and free as a prairie pony, and his rough edges had troubled Ma since the moment they met.

But now that had changed. Maybe it was the

passage of time, or the birth of baby Charles, or perhaps she was just grateful for the help Horace was providing them. Maybe Ma even saw how relieved Bill was to have another man from his own family on the farm. Whatever the reason, Ma had begun to warm up to Horace. She listened along with everyone else when he told his horse stories, instead of making a disapproving face. She went out to watch him trot Rogue around the stable while standing on the horse's back. And when Horace offered to teach Bill the same trick, she made a clucking noise and shook her head, but she didn't really seem upset. Horace was family now, in actions as well as blood. He had come through for the Codys when they needed him. The very fact of it warmed Bill to his toes like a steaming cup of tea on a rainy day.

And at last, with two of them sharing the work, there was time in the day to relax. Not much, of course. But here and there a gap in activity would come, and Bill would steal away to the stable to pamper Prince, or to reread the letter from Joe that had arrived several days ago.

He was sitting on the grass behind the cabin, leaning up against a fence rail, when Julia approached him. Though there were about fifty acres of grassland stretching off to his right, Bill made a point of moving over slightly, making room for his sister to sit next to him.

"From Joe?" asked Julia, nodding toward the letter.

She already knew that it was.

"Yeah," Bill said. "You want to read it?" Julia had not had a special friend her own age in Le Claire, and she had never received her own letter.

"Sure," Julia said, taking the letter from Bill.

The letter talked about steamboats, and who was piloting what, and what boats were the finest. It talked about Iowa and the Mississippi River and what mills were still running and which had burned down. Joe asked about Indians and buffalo and Bill's horse, Prince. In short, he sounded exactly like Joe Barnes. It was both comforting and sad to Bill to picture Joe living precisely the same life they'd shared just over a year ago.

Steamboats and rapids pilots seemed like a vague memory to Bill now. And Joe's questions about Indians and buffalo made him seem just plain inexperienced. Bill had to remind himself that there was a time before he had ever seen Indians, a time when the prospect of seeing herds of buffalo on their wagon trip had seemed thrilling.

Now Kansas Territory was Bill's reality. It was neither as exciting as Bill and Joe had imagined it would be nor as boring as Bill's chore list might make it sound. It was different, that was all. More harsh, more unforgiving, and more dangerous than Bill had thought, and more rewarding than anything he'd ever experienced. It was Kansas Territory. Even with his improved writing skills, Bill knew he could never really convey that to Joe. There were some things Joe just wasn't going to be able to understand about Bill anymore.

Julia finished reading the letter, folded it, and handed it back to Bill.

"Well," she said. "It's funny. He sounds so . . . young. I don't mean that as an insult, mind."

Bill knew exactly what Julia meant. He was relieved she felt the same way.

"No, I know how you mean it," he said quickly. "It's like everything's the same for him as it always was. And everything is so different for us."

"He probably can't even help it," Julia added. "Nobody who hasn't been where we've been could really understand the way things are for us now. What's happened to us. Nobody but a Cody can understand the kinds of problems we have here in Kansas."

Nobody but a Cody. Like a gust of wind on a calm day, the realization hit Bill. Nobody but a Cody could understand the Codys right now, and nobody but Julia could fully understand Bill. They shared the same history. The same fears. Here Bill had spent all this time trying to avoid talking to Julia, trying to keep her away from him so he could find a real friend he could talk to, and of course she was the one person he could talk to more easily than anyone else, because he didn't have to explain a thing. She knew it all already.

With a chuckle he realized they were sitting in the backyard. Where Miss Lyons had told him to look. Right again.

"What's so funny?" Julia asked.

"Nothin'," Bill replied. "Just thinking."

"About what? Or are you gonna scold me for asking?" Julia asked, only half joking.

Bill was quiet for a moment. Then he turned to his sister.

"Do you think Pa gets scared?" Bill asked. Julia looked at him for a moment in surprise.

"Course he does," she said. "I don't see how he could avoid it."

"Why do you say that?" Bill asked.

"Well, look at everything he's got going on. He's got the claim here, which until a few months ago he was in charge of running. He's got Ma, and us girls, and now the baby to get fed and kept safe. The animals that need feeding and tending, the crops, the locals, the ruffians. His business in Grasshopper Falls, now. The politics. Pa's got a family that he loves and a whole mess of problems. I wouldn't know what to make of him if he didn't feel afraid once in a while."

Julia paused and looked at Bill.

"I'd have to say I don't think I'd trust anyone to take care of me unless I knew that deep down, they could feel just as scared as I do sometimes. That's how I know a person is really paying attention."

She didn't say anything else, and Bill did little

more than nod. When she got up to go fetch a few buckets of water for Ma, Bill went with her. Carrying the load between them got the chore done twice as fast.

It seemed far too soon for the Hathaways to be leaving, but they were packed and ready. Nate was taking Miss Lyons's trunk to Leavenworth City. She would ride Bonnie there herself, to begin her new life as Mrs. Hook. She rode with the Hathaways to the Cody cabin, so they could all take their leave together.

"I'm glad we have the chance to say a proper good-bye," Miss Lyons said to Bill. They had gone into the stable to fetch a hoof pick, as Miss Lyons suspected Bonnie had a pebble wedged into her shoe.

"Yes, ma'am," said Bill. He couldn't think of anything better to say, and his voice sounded funny because of the little lump in his throat.

"You're an exceptional boy, Bill Cody," Miss Lyons said. "I expect great things from you, do you know that?"

Bill nodded. He didn't know anything of the sort.

"I want you to remember something," she said. "You have a true instinct for what is right. If you follow your heart, you will always do the right thing. I think you will find you always have the answer within you. Just have faith and let it come."

"Yes, ma'am," Bill said. There was so much more he wanted to say. But he couldn't.

Miss Lyons glanced at Horace's sleeping roll, lying in the stable corner.

"Your cousin is staying for a spell, to give you a hand with things?" she asked.

"That's right," Bill replied. "He's staying through harvest time."

"You asked for help, and you got it," she said.

"I did," Bill said. "You were right. I figure you're right about most everything."

Miss Lyons laughed.

"Oh, you'd be surprised, Bill, the number of times I'm dead wrong. But yes, this time I was right. You're going to be fine, now."

"I expect I will," Bill said.

There were voices outside the stable. Everyone had come out of the cabin.

"Sounds like it's time," Miss Lyons said.

"Sounds like it," Bill replied. Were those tears in his eyes? Horrified, he turned away and ran his hands over a rope and halter hanging from a peg.

"Gotta mend that," he said, touching the rope. Then he faked a sneeze and quickly rubbed his face. Miss Lyons took the opportunity to fuss with one of her riding boots.

"I'm ready," she said a few moments later, straightening.

They walked outside, a used-to-be boy and his used-to-be teacher.

Doc Hathaway had already climbed up onto the seat of the covered wagon and taken up the reins. Mrs. Hathaway was giving baby Charles one last kiss on the head. The scene was a familiar one from Iowa, a loaded wagon ready to make its way toward a new life. Only this time it was the Codys who were staying behind.

Martha and Miss Lyons were hugging tightly. *Martha is going to miss her too*, Bill thought. It wasn't often he had much in common with Martha, but he could understand her sadness.

A moment later Miss Lyons was up in Bonnie's saddle. She and the Hathaways would travel along the Fort Riley Road as far as the Leavenworth ferry. There the Hathaways would buy ferry tickets, and Corporal Curtis was to meet and escort Miss Lyons several miles downriver to Leavenworth City. She wasn't exactly going to the ends of the earth. And if Julia eventually did go to school in Leavenworth, Bill would be almost assured of seeing Miss Lyons again. Though it might be many months . . . Bill issued three straight fake sneezes, and pulled a handkerchief out of his pocket to blow his nose.

It seemed to take a long time, but finally the little group was ready to go. Ma held baby Charles in one arm and waved with the other. Julia held on to Mary Hannah's and Nellie's hands, keeping them well away from the wagon wheels. Eliza Alice was holding Martha's hand, the two of them looking quite bereft, and they walked after the wagon for thirty or forty feet, continuing to wave and call until it got too hard to keep up.

Now the Hathaways and Miss Lyons were joining the folks Bill knew primarily through memory. He sighed quietly. Good-byes were difficult. But it did seem that for everyone he watched leave his life, there was always a new person to take the place. And when they reappeared in his life, he thought, glancing at Horace going into the stable, it was like coming home all over again.

Bill is sitting up high in the driver's seat of a magnificent Concord stagecoach. He is admiring the team of horses harnessed to the coach. They are tall and muscular bays with gleaming coats and high proud heads. Inside the coach his ma, baby Charles, and his sisters are seated comfortably. They are chattering excitedly, one talking over the next, and their voices blend into a single, pleasant song. Turk is running alongside the coach, his tongue hanging happily out of the side of his mouth. Prince, wearing neither bridle nor saddle, follows them at a brisk trot.

They are making a familiar trip. Perhaps it is to Fort Leavenworth, or to the ferry leading to Missouri. Or perhaps they are making a trip back home to Iowa. Bill isn't exactly sure. He knows only that he has been down this road many, many times before.

It has been raining, and there are muddy patches. The sky is still dark gray, and it looks like a thunderstorm may be heading their way. Or possibly a cyclone—the conditions are right for it, and it is the time of year when twisters frequently stampede through the plains. Bill is trying to watch the road and sky at the same time, keeping the coach going at a controlled pace. But his eyelids are drooping and his head feels heavy. He fears he may fall asleep at any moment. He nods off for a quick second, then jerks upright. Someone is trying to pull the reins out of his hands.

Bill tightens his grip on the reins and hangs on tight. He turns to his left, where his sister Julia is sitting next to him. She gestures to Bill to hand the reins over to the person on his right. The horses, sensing a struggle over the reins, are confused. Two slow up, and two more try to go faster. The coach veers slightly to the right. If they keep up this way, they'll go off the road.

The more Bill hangs on to the reins, the more insistently they are tugged away from him. He hears a window sliding open in the coach, and the voices of his family come through louder and more clearly. Again he hears Julia urging him to hand over the reins.

Suddenly Bill obeys and lets the reins be taken from his hands by the person sitting to his right. It is a shadowy figure he is not sure he recognizes. It might be Pa, or Horace. It might even be Miss Lyons. He can't make *it out. The figure has the reins in both hands now. He straightens the team out, and the Concord is back on the road. The figure is driving the team with command and experience. Bill knows this driver can be trusted.*

Bill gives in to the tug of his chin on his chest. He allows his head to drop, his eyes to close. He bends forward, then tips left until his head rests comfortably on Julia's shoulder. Dimly, he feels warmth as she wraps part of her blanket around him and draws him closer. It is such a relief to be a passenger for a while, such a relief to have given the reins to someone else. Now he can doze for as long as he likes, safe in the knowledge that he and his family are in good hands.

Snug in his bed in the cozy loft, Bill took a deep breath and turned over onto his stomach. The pillow was cool and soft under his cheek, and the night was perfectly quiet.

Moments later, he was deep in peaceful sleep.

AFTERWORD

★   ★   ★

Readers familiar with the first two books in the Buffalo Bill series, *To the Frontier* and *One Sky Above Us*, already know that Bill Cody was a real boy, and that his story is a true one.

After the Codys moved from Le Claire, Iowa, to Kansas Territory in 1854, they found themselves in the middle of an explosive conflict over the issue of slavery. Though Bill's Pa had hoped simply to farm in Kansas, and stay out of politics altogether, he soon learned that those who had not already chosen sides would be forced to do so. When Pa was stabbed by proslaver Charlie Dunn in September 1854, Bill's role in the family's life changed dramatically.

By his ninth birthday, Bill was required to take

a leading role on the farm and shoulder the lion's share of the responsibility himself. For the twenty-first-century nine-year-old such a feat might sound outrageous. But in Bill's time, children of settler families made significant contributions to the family beginning as early as three or four years old. Bill and his sisters were accustomed to hard work. But the hardships forced on them by Pa's absence were difficult to bear, as we see in the autobiographies written in later years by Bill and his sister Julia.

The major events and characters in this book are all based on fact. Ma and Pa did establish a school in their old shanty, and Miss Jennie Lyons did take on the job of schoolteacher until proslavers harassed and threatened the school. Miss Lyons did marry H. M. Hook, who later became the first mayor of Cheyenne, Wyoming. And the Codys' youngest son, Charles Whitney, was born in Kansas Territory on May 10, 1855.

The border ruffians continued to harass the Codys in Pa's absence. The story of the family making noise in heavy boots and claiming Jim Lane was in the house is true, though Corporal Curtis is a fictional character.

As Bill's story continues, the tension that will ultimately lead to the Civil War continues in what historians were later to call Bleeding Kansas. Some books do refer to Isaac Cody as having shed the first blood in Kansas, calling the route to the doctor the "Cody Bloody Trail." Forced to find new ways to provide income for his family, Bill will leave home and experience some of the adventures he has previously known only in his dreams.